Looking for Marco Polo

Other Yearling Books You Will Enjoy

WHITTINGTON, *Alan Armstrong*
RALEIGH'S PAGE, *Alan Armstrong*
MATILDA BONE, *Karen Cushman*
A PICKPOCKET'S TALE, *Karen Schwabach*

Looking for Marco Polo

By Alan Armstrong

Illustrated by Tim Jessell

A Yearling Book

This is a work of fiction. All incidents and dialogue, and all characters with the exception of some well-known historical and public figures, are products of the author's imagination and are not to be construed as real. Where real-life historical or public figures appear, the situations, incidents, and dialogues concerning those persons are fictional and are not intended to depict actual events or to change the fictional nature of the work. In all other respects, any resemblance to persons living or dead is entirely coincidental.

 Published in the United States by Yearling, an imprint of Random House Children's Books, a division of Random House, Inc., New York. Originally published in hardcover in the United States by Random House Children's Books, New York, in 2009.

Visit us on the Web! www.randomhouse.com/kids

Educators and librarians, for a variety of teaching tools, visit us at www.randomhouse.com/teachers

The Library of Congress has cataloged the hardcover edition of this work as follows:
Armstrong, Alan W.
Looking for Marco Polo/by Alan Armstrong ; illustrated by Tim Jessell. — 1st ed.
p. cm.
Summary: When they lose touch with his father's Gobi Desert expedition, eleven-year-old Mark accompanies his mother to Venice, Italy, and there, while waiting for news of his father, learns about the legendary Marco Polo and his adventures in the Far East.
ISBN 978-0-375-83321-2 (trade) — ISBN 978-0-375-93321-9 (lib. bdg.) — ISBN 978-0-375-89298-1 (ebook)
1. Polo, Marco, 1254–1323?—Juvenile fiction. [1. Polo, Marco, 1254–1323?—Fiction. 2. Venice (Italy)—Fiction. 3. Voyages and travels—Fiction. 4. Italy—Fiction.] I. Jessell, Tim, ill. II. Title.
PZ7.A73352Lo 2009 [Fic]—dc22 2008008815

ISBN 978-0-375-83322-9 (trade pbk.)

Printed in the United States of America
10 9 8 7 6 5 4 3 2
First Yearling Edition 2011

Random House Children's Books supports the First Amendment and celebrates the right to read.

This book is for Devin. It owes its life to
Kate Klimo, Alfred Hart, and Martha Armstrong.
I owe mine to the original Dr. Hornaday.

How many miles to Babylon?
Ten, if your legs be long.
—child's game song

CONTENTS

Looking for Marco Polo

1

Packing Light

"Here's the scale," said Mark, setting it down on the kitchen table. He looked worried.

"Thanks, Mark," his father said, ruffling the boy's hair.

"That's all you're taking . . . for *six months*?" Mark asked as his father juggled a plastic bag from hand to hand, weighing pocketknives, tweezers, and magnifying glasses. He tossed the bag on the pile to pack.

His father smiled and nodded. "The guide who'll be taking me in said I should pack light, twenty pounds max. It'll be on my back the whole time, he said. I've gotta be able to jump quick when my camel stumbles."

Mark's father was leaving the next day to go to the Gobi Desert. The name sounded scary to Mark.

"Everything I need I'll carry on my back," his

father continued. "The guide said if I could manage more, I should plan on carrying extra water. Never enough of that on the desert."

He was a tall man with thick dark hair that was going gray. His long face was weathered, his eyes striking blue. He carried himself like a soldier. He taught anthropology and studied how the desert herders lived—personal, everyday things like what they made and used, how they washed, their jokes and songs, what they ate. Mark was entranced by his father's stories, especially the ones about kids growing up on the desert.

Mark had eyes like his father. At eleven, he was small for his age and subject to wheezing. He figured he was nowhere near as brave as his dad.

"Can't you take a Jeep?" Mark wanted to know. When he and his mother had gone with him to study the Native American herders in Arizona, they'd traveled by Jeep.

"Nope. No roads, no gas stations—there's nothing out there," his father explained. "Besides, my project is to meet and live with the desert people like Marco Polo did. I'll be traveling with the herders, sleeping in their yurts—the round tents they fold up and move as they follow the flock. All around there'll be empty space, nothing but sand and sometimes thornbush."

Mark stared at his father. The man acted like he

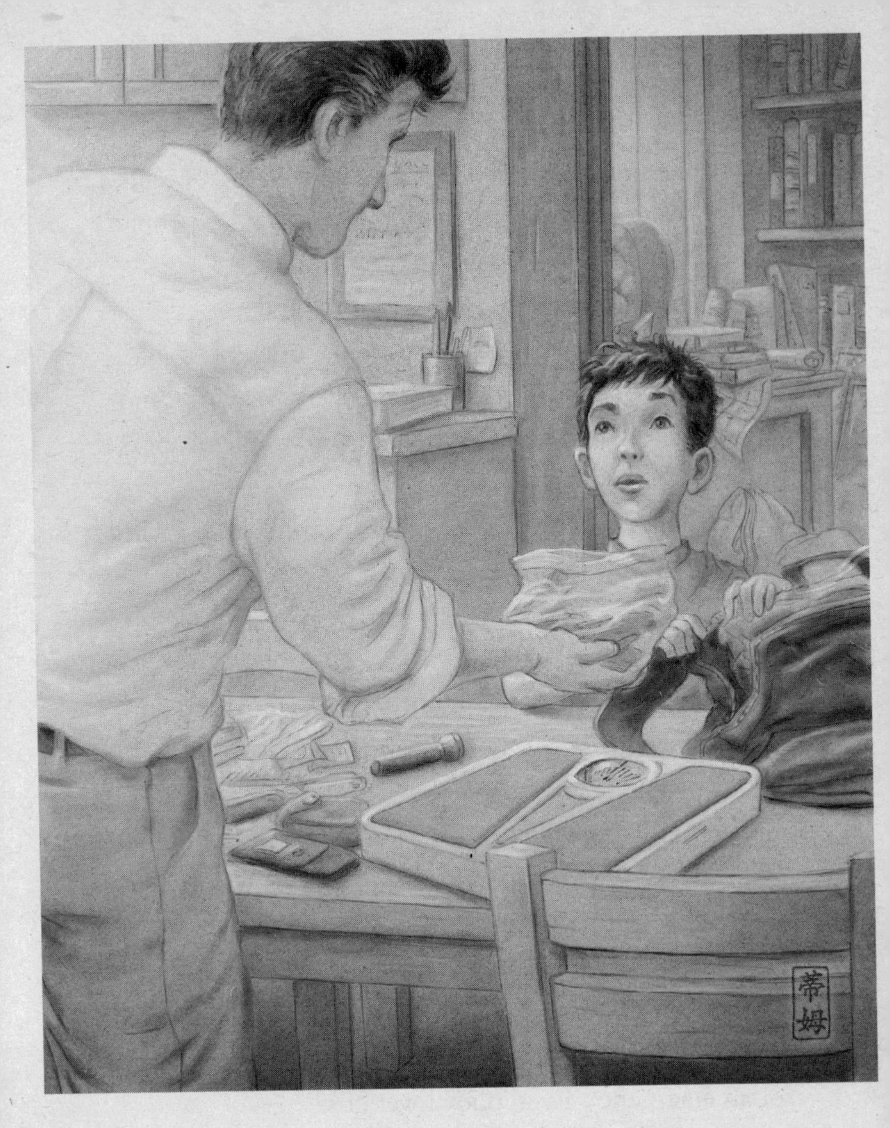

was glad it was going to be hard, like it was a test he was eager to take. It bothered Mark that he wasn't tough like that.

"What if you need something?" the boy asked.

"I'll trade for it if they have it," his father said, "stuff like the fat they mix with the boiled juice of special roots and put on their faces like sunblock."

"Won't they take money?" Mark asked.

"Desert people don't trust money unless it's gold. No place to spend it. They trade their weavings and dried meat and hides for things like metal pots and tools."

"What will you trade with?" Mark asked. "The knives and stuff in that bag?"

"No. Those are presents. I'll trade with salt. Desert people always need salt."

"You mean you're going to pay for your food and everything with *salt*?" the boy asked.

"I probably won't have to pay for food," his father replied. "I'll be their guest. Mongol herders on the Gobi don't have much, but they share what they have—even with a stranger."

He reached in his pocket and brought out two gold coins, each the size of a thumbnail. "English sovereigns," he said. "I'll carry them in the heels of my boots for an emergency. Everybody loves gold."

Mark watched his father roll his things into tight sausages and stuff them into the backpack: khaki shirts and pants, underwear, the silk T-shirt and long johns that would serve for pajamas, wool socks, a broad-brimmed canvas hat with a flap to cover the back of his neck.

"How come you squish everything up like that?" the boy asked.

"Roll your stuff tight, get the air out, saves space," his father said as he added a Swiss Army knife, a compass, ballpoint pens, matches, pouches of salt, aspirin, a sewing kit, and pads of lightweight paper to his pack. "Done!"

He stood back.

"That's it?" the boy asked.

"Yup. Let's see what it weighs."

Mark lifted the pack and put it on the scale. "Nineteen and a half pounds," he read.

"Good," said his father. "We'll top it off with the trinkets and my maps."

"No books?" Mark asked. "No flashlight, no radio?"

"Nope," said his father, stuffing in the packet of maps. "Batteries don't last long, and they're heavy. As for books, I won't have time to read.

"I've got one for you, though," he said, handing Mark a worn paperback. "*The Travels of Marco Polo.* I'll be going where he went, traveling the way he traveled. Until a hundred years ago, Marco's account was the best we had of the Gobi. I marked for you what he said about where I'll be."

The cover showed a young man struggling to hold the lead of a snarling camel in front of a squat, fierce-looking Mongol warrior in battle gear.

"Marco and Kublai Khan," his father explained. "Kublai is the emperor Marco went to meet and ended up having to help for almost twenty years."

He fastened the pack straps. "I'll write when I can," he said. "I hope you and Mom will write me a lot. Every week or so the agency in Venice that's arranged my trip will send someone out from their base near the desert. I'd love to hear from you."

Mark frowned. "How will they know where you are?"

"They know the grazing routes and where we'll stop for water. They know about how fast the animals move, so they'll always have some idea of where I am. They'll find me, don't worry. I'll be out there studying the nomads and looking for hints and traces of Marco Polo. Sleuthing beats sightseeing."

Mark nodded slowly and stared at the book in his hands. The rope Marco was holding ran through a hole in the camel's nose. The wild-eyed animal had thrown back his head and bared his teeth. Marco looked scared. Kublai looked angry. What if his father met up with someone like that who made him stay for years? He didn't like the idea of his father going off with almost nothing to a place where there wasn't even a gas station.

* * *

His father left the next day. He called when he got to Venice. Ten days later Mark and his mother got a packet of letters from him.

They wrote every other day and waited impatiently for him to answer, joking about eating grilled goat and washing with sand. After a month without any letters, they stopped joking. His mother didn't say so, but Mark could tell she was worried. And Mark was having bad dreams about being lost in a sandy wasteland.

Dear Dad,

I know you won't get this, but Mom's making us go to Venice to find you. She says in Marco Polo's time it was the greatest city in Europe. Maybe, but it means we're going to miss all the Christmas stuff here. My pack weighs nineteen pounds even with the boots Mom says I have to take because Venice is wet and mucky. It sounds really lousy. I hope we find you.

Love, Mark

2

MARCO POLO'S HILTON

"Look, Mark!" Mark's mother stopped.

He looked where she pointed, across the canal at the large reddish figure of a camel mounted over a doorway. Camels reminded him of the book his father had given him. He'd left it at home.

"Yeah," he said.

"Maybe that's like the one Marco rode," she said. "Or Dad."

Mark could tell she was trying to get him interested, but Venice was not his idea of a great place to spend Christmas.

Suddenly the sun came out and struck the side of the building where the camel was. The animal seemed to move. Mark kept staring at it over his shoulder as he walked. The alley narrowed. He teetered, then caught himself.

"I bet a lot of people fall in," he said, pointing to the canal. "No guardrails or anything!"

His mother pinched her nose. "And when they fish them out, phew!"

They were walking against the wind. His mom was dragging her suitcase. It lurched over the worn stone pavers like a boat on a tossing sea. The water beside them was dull gray with strands of green floating in it. Sometimes when a motorboat went by, its wake water lapped up. At places where the water stood ankle-deep, boards had been laid like temporary docks.

Everything looked as if it were rising right out of the water. Water lapped palace fronts of white marble and the plainer painted walls, gnawing away the stucco to the brick underneath. The tides had left lines of fuzzy green moss that shaded down to darker lines and clots of small black-shelled mussels.

As his mother stopped to check her map, people flowed past with small wheeled carts filled with groceries, laundry, wine, and flowers. There were no cars.

They went slowly along the stone lanes and dark alleys, some so narrow they had to walk single file. Their route humped, wove, and twisted, always near the milky green water. Laundry fluttered from lines and balconies overhead.

Finally they turned into a small square. Mark's

mother stopped and pointed to a battered brown door. "There. That must be it," she said.

Mark stared. "You sure? It looks like somebody's falling-down house."

"Nope. Sign says 'hotel.' "

A large lamp that looked like it had been knocked cockeyed hung over the front, ALBERGO written on the glass in faded gold.

She went up and pressed a button. Nothing happened. She waited and pressed again. Then she held the button down and began to pound. Finally the lock buzzed.

The heavy door opened into a large, dark, stone-floored room. The stones were scooped and rounded. The only thing in the room was a long sagging table against one wall. At the far end, under a small round window with bars, there were white marble stairs. It smelled old and damp, as if there'd been animals in it a long time ago. Rusted hooks and rings stuck out from the walls.

"It looks like a dungeon," Mark muttered. He shivered as the stale dankness settled on him.

His mother pointed to the stairs. They twisted up with a spindly rail on one side. A dim light showed from the landing above.

"No elevator?" Mark asked.

"Let's leave our stuff here," his mother said. "I'll get someone to bring it up."

They started up the stairs together. Mark stumbled on the fourth flight. His mother steadied him. They'd been up all night flying from Baltimore.

"You'll be okay," she told him. "Jet lag. It'll pass."

The door at the top had glass in the center with ALBERGO SAN RAFFAELLO in gold like on the lamp outside. The handle was the head of a broad-faced bearded man.

The door opened into a small, brightly lit room with mirrors and sculptures and a small reception desk. Everything was small, even the chairs. The furniture had traces of gold trim. It smelled of polish.

After she arranged things with the clerk, Mark's mother pointed him to his room. It was next to hers. His door key was attached to a heavy knot. "So you won't forget to leave it at the desk when you go out," she explained.

They went into their rooms, leaving the doors open so they could talk.

"Hey, Mom!" Mark called over. "What is this place? There's a Madonna on the wall!"

"Shhh . . . Keep it down!" his mother said as she came into his room. "Italians put up religious ornaments for a blessing. It's the custom."

Mark looked around. "Where's the bathroom?"

"Down the hall. The door marked 'WC.' We have to share it."

Mark drooped. "Share it? Who with?"

"Everyone on this floor," she said cheerfully, pointing to the other doors. "You peek out to see if the WC door is open. If it is, make a run for it before somebody beats you to it. It's kind of fun."

"Oh man," Mark muttered, feeling his way down the dark hall.

"It smells!" he exclaimed when he came out. "And there's no shower or anything!"

His mother went over and stuck her head in. "That's Venice! Seawater and sewage," she said with a shrug. "I've been in worse. For a shower you go up to the front, the door just before the reception desk."

"Not very private," Mark grumbled, flopping down on his mother's bed. "Not like a Hilton."

"Maybe it was Marco Polo's Hilton," she suggested. "Speaking of which . . ." She went and dug around in her suitcase, pulling out a book. She tossed it onto the bed next to him. "I guess you forgot this."

It was the book his father had given him, the one with Marco Polo, the grimacing camel, and the scary Kublai Khan on the cover. He'd read the first few pages and tossed it under his bed.

"I didn't forget it," he muttered. "I left it behind. I don't care about Marco Polo. I care about Dad. That's why we came. I didn't come to find out about Marco Polo. Venice smells bad." He made a face. "Even my room smells bad, and the floor's all up and down."

"Maybe you can put that in your next letter to Dad," his mother said, taking things out of her suitcase and hanging them up in the wardrobe.

"I don't have any paper. But, anyway, why bother? He's not even getting 'em!"

Mark scowled and fanned the pages of the Marco Polo book. It felt hot.

"You don't know that," said his mother.

"No closets here either," Mark complained, "just these big old boxes with doors on the front. Mine looks like it could fall over. I'm leaving my stuff in my backpack."

"Suit yourself," his mother replied as she bustled about. When she was finished, she sat down next to Mark and opened her cell phone. He knew who she was calling: the agency that had been responsible for sending his father into the unknown; the agency that didn't seem to care whether his father ever came back again or not.

"Marian Hearn here," she said into the phone. "Yes, we just arrived. Good. You have my cell phone number. Call me when you hear anything. *Anything!*"

She shut the phone and nodded firmly. "They're sending out a search party tomorrow. I knew our coming to Venice would light a fire under those people."

"Does that mean we can go home now?" Mark asked. He was only half joking.

"Oh, come on!" his mother snapped. "We're staying put right here until they find him. I'm showing up in their offices every morning until they do. Now, I'm hungry. There's a café on the corner. Let's go."

"I'm not hungry," Mark said, yawning. "I just want to stay here and sleep."

"Nope." His mother stood up and grabbed his arm. "We need to get out in the sunlight to reset our body clocks."

Mark groaned, but he knew it was useless to argue.

They dropped off their keys and started down the stairs. Mark counted. There were sixty-eight.

It was midmorning but it felt like midnight. They'd been up for thirty hours. The fast-moving clouds overhead made Mark feel dizzy. When the sun broke through, it glittered on the water. Pigeons swirling up seemed to mimic the sunlight flickering off the waves. Strings of violet and white Christmas lights hung over the narrow streets, a few with white stars in the middle. Over the shop doors there were bunches of evergreens sprayed silvery blue and tied up with what the shop

蒂姆

sold—blue shoes and handbags above a leather shop, blue-painted books above a bookshop. The bakery had sprigs of pine with blue-painted loaves of bread.

They went into the café on the corner. It was warm and steamy and fragrant. Red-skinned oranges were piled high in a wire basket on the counter. A man was slicing and juicing them in a machine that sounded like a lawn mower. The juice spurted out like lumpy blood. The man seemed to have ten hands—slicing oranges, chopping onions and garlic, shredding mozzarella, cutting up vegetables, ham, and sausages.

The food smelled good. There was music playing, something quick with violins. Suddenly Mark was hungry.

One corner of the café was filled with a round-fronted brick oven with a half-oval opening at chest height. Mark could see coals and flames. He wondered if they cooked pizza in it.

In the opposite corner there was a niche with the statue of a golden-faced woman. She was an arm's length tall. Flowers were banked up around her, so Mark couldn't make her out, but it looked as if her body had been splashed with red and black paint. She didn't look like any Madonna he'd ever seen before.

"Buon giorno," called the nodding waitress as she pointed them to a table on one side of the oven.

"Buon giorno," Mark's mother said.

"Hi," said Mark.

He sat down with his back to the oven. The heat felt good.

The woman circled back with a cup of coffee for Mark's mother and a larger cup for him filled with hot milk and a little coffee.

As the waitress put down their cups, she pointed to a large, two-handled, gold-domed pot on the counter—*"Zucchero,"* she said. The thing looked like a sports trophy.

"Sugar," Mark's mother translated.

The waitress turned quickly and yelled something to the orange-slicing man. He wasn't alarmed; he yelled back, *"Sì! Sì!,"* wiped his hands on his juice-stained apron, grabbed what looked like a canoe paddle, and hustled over to the oven to slide out a square pan bubbling over with tomato and browning cheese. It smelled wonderful.

Mark went to the counter to sugar his cup. The counterman looked up and smiled.

"Please?" Mark asked, pointing and gesturing to let the man know he wanted some of the stuff in the square pan.

"Lasagna? No, no, not yet," the man said, shaking his head. "It must ripen. We cool it, then bake it once more for *il pranzo.* You come for il pranzo—lunch—then you eat the lasagna. I save for you a big piece," he said, spreading his hands wide. "Okay?"

"Okay," said Mark. He looked in the case, then pointed to a yellow pancake. The counterman nodded happily, signaling that Mark had chosen the best thing for *la colazione*—breakfast—as he sprinkled on herbs from a big tin shaker and painted it lightly with olive oil before he slid it into the oven.

The pancake was a *frittata*—whipped egg baked with cheese and garlic and bits of ham and broccoli, his mother explained. It came with a glass of the dark red orange juice and a plate of small crescent-shaped pastries dusted white with sugar.

"Mmm," said Mark as he took a bite of frittata.

The juice was sweet. The pastries tasted like almond, their sugar dusting fine as flour.

"So what did Marco eat for breakfast?" he asked.

His mother looked up from her cup. "I don't know," she said. "Maybe a cup of hot milk, but no coffee in it, I guess, and no sugar. Maybe a small round of bread smeared with fat, and an apple. Maybe an egg or a piece of fried fish."

Mark made a face. "Fish for breakfast? Ugly!"

The waitress answered the phone in the corner. Her whole conversation was "Eh? Eh! Eh. Eh. Eh. Eh!

Eh." She was a short, round woman in worn-down bedroom slippers, a bright print dress, and a smeared blue-striped apron. Her voice went up and down like a saxophone.

When she finished the call, she shuffled over, her slippers *flap-flapp*ing with every step. Without asking, she poured more juice and put down another plate of sweet crescents. "Eh?" she said with a wink at Mark.

The two women chatted, then the waitress turned to Mark. "Why you spend Christmas in Venice?" she asked.

Mark licked the powdered sugar off his lips. "We're looking for my father," he said. "He's lost."

"Your father?" she cried. "He is lost in Venice?"

Mark's mother put in gently, "Actually, he's in the Gobi Desert, but the agency he works for is here in Venice. And he might not be lost. He's doing research with the herders, following the path your famous Marco Polo followed across the desert."

"Ah! Marco Polo!" said the waitress, seeming to swell up as she opened her arms and smiled at Mark. "Marco Polo. 'Millionaire Marco,' we call him for his big stories. He is like a sport star with us. I am sorry I cannot tell you how to find your father, but Marco Polo, he is all over Venice. Except for his body. They lost it. Give me your map. I show you where you look for Marco . . . start here, this place, where is his home—Casa Polo."

Dad,

How come you came here to go to the desert? Did you go by boat? Mom's been showing me where you are on the map. There's no TV in my room, not even a radio. Venice is wet and smelly. Some of the buildings lean like they might fall over—which Mom says is because everything is built on poles stuck in the mud. Why did anyone ever bother coming to this place? I can see why Marco Polo left. Breakfast was OK. What do you get for breakfast? Do they make coffee where you are? I hope we hear something about you today.

Love, Mark

3

Marco Polo's Pillow

As they set out from Signora Eh's café, a sharp breeze made them hunker into their coats and bury their hands.

"Hats would be good," Mark's mother said.

"I bet Dad wouldn't wear one," Mark said, setting his face and squinting. The cold wind made him tear.

"Bet he would," his mom said, rubbing her ears. "Something woven out of camel's hair like the herders wear."

They heard the Christmas market before they saw it, a hum of happy people. Around the edges there were jugglers and clowns and men painted gold all over standing like statues before dishes for tips. Farther along a troupe of mimes in white pretended to sing opera without making a sound. From the way the actors gestured, Mark could follow the story. People around him were swaying to the imagined music.

There was a stand for mittens, scarves, and hats. Mark's mother stopped and quickly bought a beret for herself and a bright red wool watch cap like sailors wear. She held it out. Mark shrugged and pulled it on.

A tanned old man in a black hat was selling flowers from a rickety handcart he must have made and painted himself. It had the picture of a smiling golden-faced Madonna on the front. She was surrounded by strings of red and yellow flowers, blue leaves, and grinning red snakes. Some of the man's teeth were gold. He was no taller than Mark, but he was broad and strong. His hat was dusty; his gray shirt was mended and stained. Mark noticed he wore more shirts underneath.

He had roses. Mark's mother leaned over and sniffed.

"Ah," she said with a sigh.

"From Sicily," the man said proudly. "Where I from. At Christmas, roses in Sicily, so I bring here."

"Wonderful. Just what we need," she said. "Six, please."

"For your room," she said, handing them to Mark. "I read somewhere that in the old days Venetian innkeepers put flowers in the rooms to freshen things. Now yours will smell like Christmas in Sicily—or springtime in Baltimore. Sniff!" she urged.

Mark did. "Thanks."

The old man beamed. "*Buone, eh?*—Good?"

Mark nodded. *"Grazie,"* he said.

"Prego," replied the flower-seller with a polite nod.

"He can't make much doing that, can he?" Mark asked as they walked into the buzzing warren of stands and tables. "I mean, he must be poor."

"Looks to me like he knows how to be happy with what he's got," his mother replied. "It's a gift few people have."

The square was filled with vendors' tables under gaudy striped umbrellas. One table had rows of what his mother said were *santons*—carefully painted hand-sized clay figures of Joseph, Mary, the wise men, the shepherds, and all the animals for crèches. The next stand was for puppets. Over it there was a large, sly-looking Puss in Boots in a shiny blue satin suit with silver fur cuffs and a jaunty black plumed hat. He was holding a seaman's map in one paw, a globe in the other.

The table that stopped Mark had small things from China, tiny carvings of animals and people.

"Looks like the kind of stuff Marco Polo might have brought back," his mother said.

There was a chipped green and white porcelain

box. It was the size of a small shoe box decorated with fierce-headed purple and red dragons, their blue tongues curling out. The top was slightly scooped.

"It's a Chinese pillow," his mother explained. "Marco Polo might have slept on one."

Mark put it up against the back of his head.

"How do you sleep on it?" he asked. "It's hard."

"Maybe you should try," his mother said, motioning to the dealer.

"For your Marco Polo dreams," she said with a smile as she bought it.

Mark was amazed. His mother rarely bought souvenirs, and she was really careful about money. It wasn't cheap. It looked old enough to have really belonged to Marco. "I'll try it," he said.

They bought bags of apricots and dates and ate them as they walked, spitting out the pits.

They approached what looked like a low white pyramid with a flattened top.

"The Rialto Bridge," Mark's mother said. "It's the main bridge over the Grand Canal, the great highway of Venice."

Tides of people floated up the layers of steps to the top, where they could look down on boats of all sizes and colors. A bright green garbage scow moved slowly under a cloud of screaming gulls.

The sun flickered above slate gray clouds, faster moving and darker and colder-looking than the ones they'd noticed earlier. Bells clanged the quarter hour, some five minutes before, some five minutes after, so all along there was music like the choppy waves. Men sculled by in gondolas, calling as they stroked. The water churned with the wakes of tour boats, outboards, floating buses called *vaporettos,* and taxis.

Near the bridge they stopped for coffee and hot chocoate: boiled milk in a heavy blue cup with a cube of chocolate on a stick laid alongside. Mark twirled the chocolate in the steaming white until it turned brown. It was thick and sweet.

He couldn't help himself: he slurped up a long hot sip. He looked over at his mother, expecting a scold about manners. She just shook her head and smiled.

"Oh man!" he sighed, wriggling with pleasure. "Why can't we get cocoa like this at home?"

"I guess for the same reason we can't get coffee like this," his mother said, holding up her tiny cup. "It must be the water."

"Yeah. Seawater with green stuff floating in it," Mark said. "That's what we need back home."

In the open-sided market below, a large black fish had been gutted and lopped into steaks and then put back together. The table was gooey with scales, slime, and blood. The tiny, bent-over, blood-spattered fishwoman sold her fish section by section, down to the tail, and, as they watched, she sold that too, along with the head.

Afterward they walked single file following arrows marked CA POLO along a narrow canal, then a narrow *calle,* crossing several small bridges humped just enough to allow a gondola to pass under. Laundry hung out over the smaller lanes. When the sun shone, the drying jeans, whites, and bright shirts flapped like flags.

"The map says that's it," his mother said, pointing to a wall with a marble arch.

Mark stood back and squinted to take in the wall, the arch, and the surroundings. "That?" he said as he rubbed his arms. "That's Marco Polo's house?"

"What's left of it," his mother said. "Cold?" she asked.

"I'm okay." Mark was an only child and his parents worried about him too much, particularly his mother. But he did feel odd. He shook himself like a dog shaking off wet. He couldn't explain it, but he felt as if he were in the presence of something alive that he couldn't see.

Is this what Dad meant about hints and traces? he wondered.

"It says in the guidebook," his mother said, "that Marco's house was torn down after a fire to make way for the theater. It mentions the arch, so I guess that's the one he walked under the night he got back from China. Did you read that part in the book?"

"Yeah," Mark said. It was the only part he had read: the beginning, telling about Marco's coming home after his travels. Mark thought it was strange that a story about travels should begin with the coming-home part.

The stone arch was carved with circles of flowers, shields, figures of lizard-looking beasts, and something with the head of an eagle and the body, hind legs, and tail of a lion.

Mark went over and stood under it. He stretched out his arms and measured the opening. It was four stretched-out-Marks wide. "Marco says he and his father and his uncle arrived with a donkey and a big

蒂姆

dog," he explained. "I'm just checking to see if they could all have fit through. I guess they could."

He turned and looked around the small square. "Do you think it looks the same now as it did then?" he asked.

His mother nodded. "Pretty much."

"That must be where he went to get water." Mark pointed to the wellhead. It came up to his waist and looked like the top of a column, only it was hollow. It was the length of a man across.

"If you run your hands over the stone," his mother said, "you might be able to feel where the lion's head was. It says in the guidebook that in Marco's time all the wellheads in Venice had carved lions' heads on them, but then foreign soldiers came and knocked them off."

Mark's scalp tingled.

Maybe I'm touching what Marco Polo touched.

"Was the water salty?" he asked.

"It wasn't a well," his mother explained. "The space under this paving was a cistern, maybe still is. The paving was laid on a slant, so rainwater drained into it, water from the roofs too."

"Did they drink it?" Mark asked.

His mother nodded.

Mark scrunched up his face. "Along with dead pigeons and all the other stuff that must have fallen in?"

"I don't know," she said. "Maybe they boiled it."

There was an iron grating over the top.

"They don't use it anymore, right?" Mark asked, leaning over and staring down.

"I don't think so," his mother replied.

Mark called down, "Hi!"

He waited a long moment.

"I heard back!" he said, straightening up.

They headed back to their hotel, twisting along canals and stitching over bridges. On the way they passed the big museum. It was open.

His mother pointed to the sign. "*Mondo di Marco Polo*—Marco Polo's World. Want to go in?" she asked.

Mark sagged. "Maybe later, Mom," he said. "I'm tired."

"Come on," she urged. "A quick walk through. Five minutes."

The rooms were large and dark, with tall ceilings. The first was filled with huge dark globes of the world mounted in gilded frames. Some of the globes were as tall as a man. There were cases of books laid open. Pictures and maps were hung all the way up to the ceiling. Staring up, Mark felt woozy. His legs were heavy.

The next room had a scale model of a black Venetian war galley with manikins on the benches—two to a bench, twenty-five benches on each side, with an ax and spear beside every one, sharp and ready for battle. The figure of a boy in a blue jacket sat in the stern with a drum, beating time for the rowers. The prow ended in an iron beak shaped like a dragon's head.

"They were paid," his mother translated from the sign. "These rowers weren't slaves like the Roman galley slaves. For the Venetians, being a rower was a good job. It says the point at the front was for holing the enemy."

"What's holing?" Mark wanted to know.

"Ramming—poking a hole in the enemy boat to sink it," she answered.

Mark pointed to the figure of the boy at the stern. "That kid's been beating his drum for a long time."

In the next room there was the standing figure of a Mongol warrior in quilt armor and a metal helmet with broad gold wings. He stood holding a spear beside a pony.

Mark went and stood beside the warrior. They were the same size. "Those soldiers were grown-ups, right?" he called to his mother.

"Yes," she answered. "People are bigger now. Better diet."

On the walls there were racks of Mongol lances,

each with a vicious hook just below the point. There were rows of shields made from woven reeds, the fronts covered with brass and beaten gold and decorated with black writing. In the cases there were dozens of battle helmets, each one with what looked like a vase on one side.

On the way out his mother pointed to the displays of open books. "Marco's book in French and Latin, the earliest printed ones," she said. "The ones over there, the ones written out by hand, they came first."

"Mom," Mark groaned, "I've got museum feet. . . ."

She looked at her watch. "Time for il pranzo," she announced. "Can you make it back to the signora's for some of that lasagna before we nap?"

Remembering the bubbling pan of cheese and tomato, Mark brightened. "Sure!" he said.

Just before the bridge to their *campo* his mother stopped them in front of a shop. The sign said IL PAPIRO. "Paper," she explained. "You need some for your letters to Dad."

"Aw, Mom . . ."

"One minute!"

The shopkeeper's face was a round of pink under a big black fur hat. She wore a neck-to-ankles cocoon of dark red wool. She nodded and smiled as Mark's mother stepped in, Mark lagging behind with a sour look.

"So what you need?" the woman asked, holding up a sign in English:

We provide—
Papers of every kind
Calligraphy scripts
Handwriting analysis
Palm reading
Tourist advice
Toilet—1 euro

"He needs paper for letters," Mark's mom said.

"This is good, writing letters," the woman exclaimed as she wormed past boxes and displays to a shelf, "but first you must gather ideas. You must write down what surprises—quick, before it is ordinary.

"Here—this will fit your pocket," she said, handing Mark a ballpoint and a small red leather booklet. "Try the pen on it. See? Good, the paper! Feel how it welcomes the pen! This is important: a writer's paper should never fight the hand! So you write your first book! And—see?—you can tear out sheets for mail."

Dear Dad,

Mom got the people at the agency to send out some people to look for you. I hope they find you soon. She showed me the Gobi on the map. It's colored tan, which means it's really dry. Mom's worried because of no letters, but the agency chief says he's sure you're OK because the last team met some other herders who didn't say anything was wrong except the water had moved. There's water everywhere here. The roads are water. Our hotel is old and smelly. Everything here is really old with a lot of fancy stuff hung on it. Nothing is new. The lady at the restaurant told us where Marco Polo's house was, so we went there, but it burned down a long time ago. On the way Mom bought me a pillow like he used. It's hard as a rock. I stood under the arch he went under when he came home. They named the airport for him but they lost his body. Mom read in the guidebook that most Venetians didn't wear underwear. The museum didn't have any. The woman where we bought this paper said we must be Americans because of our shoes. "For practical," she said. It's the boots Mom makes us wear. Nobody here wears things like you're going moose hunting. She read my palm for free. She says I'm going exploring. I'm keeping the notebook she sold us in my pocket to write you notes for when I see you. It's red leather. It cost a lot. People here don't go fast, or push, and lots of them smile when they look at you. There are no joggers and no black people. From the looks of the water, don't eat the fish, but the other stuff is OK. What do you eat? Mom says goat and a lot of cheese made from sheep and goat milk. She says we're going to get some to try. Ropes and life preservers are hanging all over this place so a lot of people must fall in. The fire truck is a boat. Mom says you're wearing a camel-hair hat. Are you? We saw a camel. Mom bought me a red one to wear—a hat, not a camel, but I bet you could get one here. This place is all shops and water.

Your son, Mark

4

The Wheezing Sickness

Maybe it was the long trip without sleep. Maybe he got it wandering in the cold damp of Venice. Whatever it was, that night it got him. Mark woke up coughing. He couldn't get his breath. He banged on his mother's door.

"Mom, I can't breathe," he wheezed. "It feels like somebody's standing on my chest."

His mother felt his head and listened to his chest. They tried the usual remedies—breathing over a sink of steaming hot water, rubbing Vicks on his chest and neck. Nothing helped.

She went to the office and roused the night clerk.

Mark's door was open.

"He's sick!" she said. "My boy is sick. Get a doctor, please! Quickly, a doctor! He's having trouble breathing."

Her voice had scare in it. The way she sounded made Mark scared.

"You want . . . you want a doctor to come here, to this place, Madam?" the clerk stammered. "No, you must go to the hospital. It is best, the hospital."

"Look! He's in no condition to go outside and ride in a boat," she snapped. "I want a doctor to come here."

"The hospital is close, Madam," the clerk pleaded. "I summon the rescue boat."

"The hotel does not have a doctor on call?"

"No, Signora."

She hurried back to Mark's bedside with her notebook and mobile phone. "I'm calling an army doctor here, an old friend of Dad's. They were in the Gulf War together. Let's see if he'll come."

Mark was struggling to suck in air. It sounded like there was a whistle trapped in his chest.

The phone rang for a long time. She was about to quit when the doctor answered. "Doctor Hornaday, this is Marian, Marian Hearn. Listen, I'm sorry to bother you so late, but I'm here with our son, and he's having an asthma attack. He's coughing—can't get his breath.

"No. The clerk says we should go to the hospital, but . . . You'll come? Oh, wonderful, Doc. Thank you!"

Mark was sitting up in bed, head to knees, hacking and panting, when the buzzer sounded.

His mother left his door open when she went to the reception area to greet the doctor. Mark could see into the hallway.

It took a long time, but at last the doctor appeared, out of breath from climbing the sixty-eight steps.

Mark's mother held out both hands in greeting. "Thanks for coming!"

Dr. Hornaday was a tall black man with a tightly clipped mustache. His forehead gleamed. Mist had caught on his dark felt hat and in his eyebrows. His eyebrows were thick and gray like pads of steel wool.

"It's been a long time. Good to see you," he said in a deep voice as he unwrapped his red wool scarf and tapped his hat against his coat to get the water off. His hair was like his eyebrows. He carried a scuffed black doctor's case.

Behind him limped a large black long-haired dog. His head came to the doctor's waist. His coat was matted and wet. He shook himself hard, making his chain collar and tags clank like somebody emptying a box of silverware into a drawer.

The dog's big shake sent drops flying. Fluffed up, he looked huge. His paws were the size of Mark's hands. When he walked, his claws clicked on the floor. He was panting from the climb, his long wet tongue gleaming bluish black over his big white teeth.

Mark's mother was surprised to see the dog. The night clerk was terrified. His mouth went wide like a clown's as he flapped his arms wildly to wave the animal away.

"*Fuori! Fuori!* Outside! Outside! *Non e permesso!* We do not allow dogs!" he squealed, hurrying behind his desk. "It is not permitted!"

The dog smiled, woofed hello, and wagged. The swipe of his wag cleared the brochures and tourist ads off the side table.

"I'm sorry, Signore," the doctor replied as he stooped to pick up the wet brochures, "but this is no ordinary dog—he's my buddy. I can't travel the dark alleys of Venice at night without Boss. He's my eyes, my map, and my protection. He's not dangerous unless provoked. But then, of course . . . Well, I'm sure you understand."

"Come mai!" the clerk exclaimed, throwing up his hands and scuttling back to his sleeping closet. He slammed the door and locked it.

Mark had never had a dog. He couldn't take his eyes off Boss. The dog stared back as he shuffled and shifted beside the doctor and finally sat down to scratch. Adding to the clanking of his collar and tags was the *thump-thump-thump* as his scratch paw hit the floor. Mark was sure he could feel the beats. He figured the dog weighed more than he did, one hundred pounds at least. Boss's ears were black triangles, cocked up and shifting, following everything as he looked around. They were silky-looking, delicate, seashell pink inside.

Mark was so busy staring he forgot about coughing.

Boss lurched up and shuffled noisily into his room. He put his big blunt muzzle on the bed. Without thinking, Mark put out his hand. The dog laid his head on it. The boy started, but he left his hand where it was. The dog's head was warm and comforting.

"Huh," said the doctor, following his dog. "I never saw him do that before."

"He's allergic to most animals!" Mark's mother said warily.

"We'll see," said the doctor, turning to Mark. "Hello. I'm Doctor Hornaday."

The doctor's eyes were large and calm. Mark nodded and tried to say hello back, but a cough ripped through him.

"Call me Doc," said the man with a smile. "Take off your top so I can listen to your breathing."

He wore a black turtleneck under a tweed jacket. His pants were dark corduroys. A stethoscope hung around his neck. He took a pressed white handkerchief from his breast pocket, shook it open, and wiped his face. Then he pulled on thin rubber gloves. They made his hands look as if they'd been dipped in milk.

"You afraid of what I've got?" Mark coughed.

"No," said the doctor gravely. "I do this to make you afraid of what *I've* got."

"You can't make me afraid!" Mark said.

Hornaday smiled. "I'm glad. I didn't think I could."

Boss thumped his tail. It was as long as Mark's arm and twice as big around. Mark caught a whiff of his warm, wet dog smell. It was a good, comfortable smell, strong like a horse. The dog was watching everything.

Dr. Hornaday bent down, pressing the warm stethoscope to Mark's chest. He smelled of damp wool and soap. His hands were warm. They trembled a little.

"Okay. Open wide and stick out your tongue so I can check your throat." He used a flat wooden stick to hold Mark's tongue down as he aimed a small flashlight at the back of his throat.

"How does it look?" Mark asked when Hornaday finished.

"Okay. No sign of infection. Now lie back and make yourself comfortable while I take your tempera-

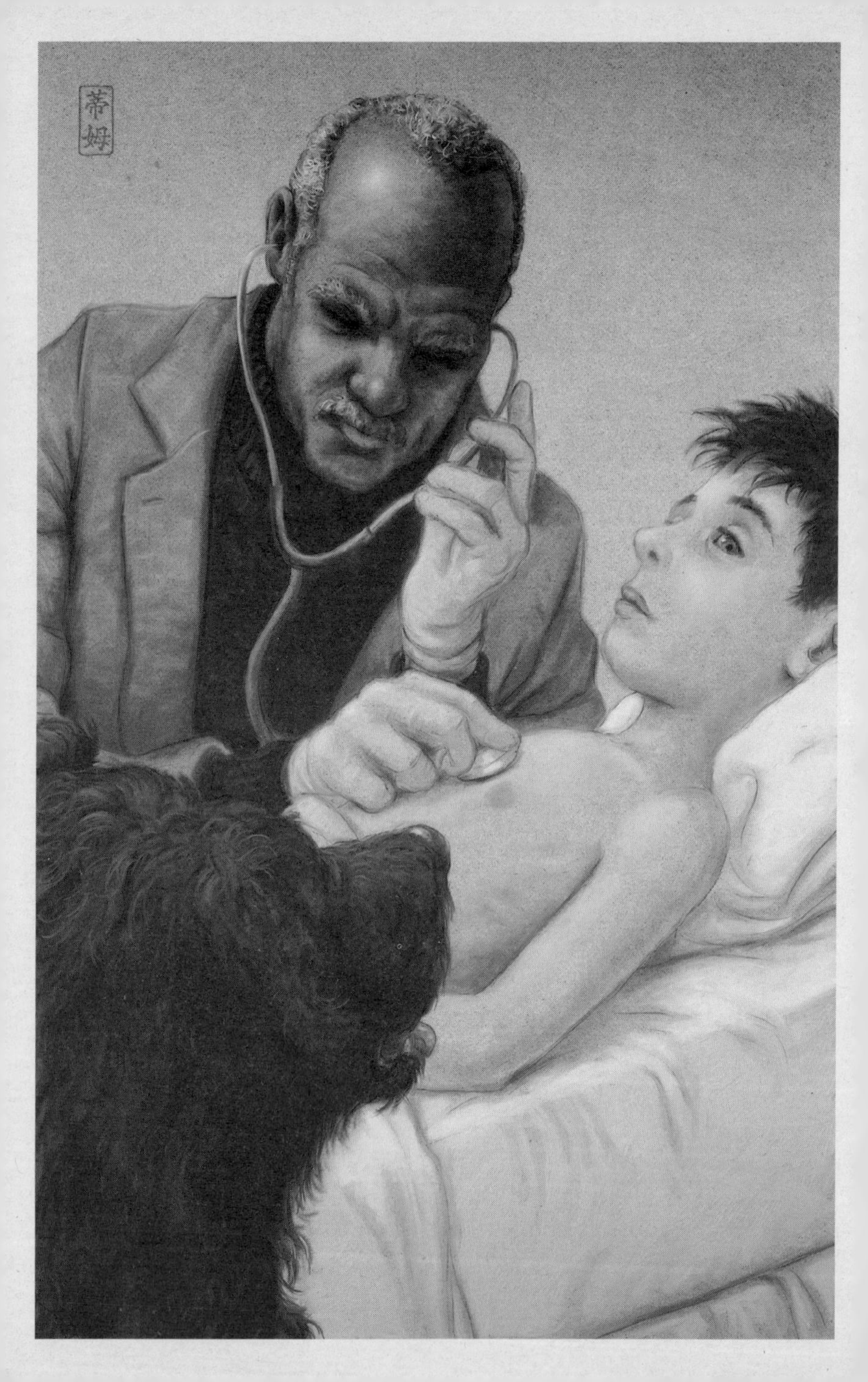
蒂姆

ture and check your blood pressure. Keep this in your mouth until the bell rings," he said as he handed Mark the thermometer.

He wrapped a pad tight around Mark's upper arm and began squeezing the bulb pump.

"What's my temperature?" Mark asked when Hornaday took out the thermometer.

"Normal. Looks to me like your mom's right. You've got what the Greeks called the wheezing sickness: asthma. You've had it before?"

Mark nodded. "Yeah, but never this bad."

Hornaday smiled. "We'll take care of it. I'm going to give you some medicine to open things up. It may make you see things, but you know, people have discovered important things in their visions."

Boss caught Mark's eye and blinked slowly.

Doc turned to Mark's mother. "Any medicines he should avoid?"

"No," she said.

"Good," said the doctor. "So it would be all right if I put him on a machine to start him on some things to calm down his breathing tubes?"

"Yes," she answered in a small voice.

"Okay with you?" he asked Mark.

"Yeah," he said, panting.

Mark's mother watched, hands to her cheeks, as

the doctor opened his case. It was like a toolbox with compartments for different-sized tapes and bandages, medicines, scissors, needles. He lifted out splints and wraps, then a small white box with a clear plastic tube. He plugged in the box, pulled the cap off the tube, and attached a soft cup with silver scales and black dot eyes that made it look like a fish head.

Hornaday poured in medicine and turned it on. It started whirring. When a white mist came out, he handed Mark the cup. "I know it looks a little silly, but push the fish head to your nose and mouth and breathe in. The mist will open things up. Try it for a few minutes, then we'll see how you do on your own."

Mark was breathing better by the time the mist stopped and the doctor pulled off the mask.

Mark's mother yawned widely. Too late, she tried to cover her mouth.

"The medicine's going to make him wakeful for a while," Doc said. "Boss and I will stay with him until he goes to sleep. Go back to bed. He'll be all right."

Boss looked up and seemed to smile.

"I should stay," she said.

"Your boy will be all right," the doctor said again.

"You sure?" she asked.

"Yes," said Hornaday in a firm voice that made Mark sure too.

"We'll talk," the doctor continued. "Mark will tell us what he wants to do in Venice. Maybe we can give him some tips. Boss and I have gone all over these hundred islands."

Boss growled a two-beat noise that sounded like "Uh-huh!"

5

The School of the Street

The medicine made Mark's heart pound. He was breathing easier, but he felt jumpy.

Hornaday bent over to listen to his chest again.

"Can I listen too?" the boy asked.

The doctor handed him the stethoscope and waited while he fit the black plugs into his ears. When Mark nodded, Hornaday began moving the other end slowly over his chest.

Mark's mouth formed an O of surprise. "It sounds like a storm in there. It's really bad, huh?"

"No," said the doctor, "just some stuff we're going to clear up."

Hornaday stood and blew out hard, as if he were blowing up a balloon.

"You try doing that. Make it hard to blow the air out; you'll force more oxygen into your lungs."

Mark tried. The doctor nodded and clapped slowly as he puffed like Mark.

"Good. Do it to a count: in two-three-four, out two-three-four. Keep time beating against the bed. Concentrate on your breathing; it'll take your mind off everything else. Get more air; you won't feel so bad. It's a kind of hypnosis."

Hornaday bent down and reached for his overcoat.

Mark stopped counting. "Hey!" he said, coughing. "You said you'd stay."

"I'm not going anywhere," Hornaday replied, pulling an orange from the coat pocket. He began to peel it. His fingers were long and slender, the color of walnut. A sharp orange smell filled the room. He handed Mark a section.

"Persians called oranges apples of Paradise. Some people think it's the fruit Eve offered Adam. They're good medicine."

As the boy chewed and swallowed, his throat cleared a little. "How do you know what Persians called oranges?" he asked.

"I once asked an old man in the bazaar for an apple of Paradise," the doctor replied. "He handed me an orange."

"Where was that?"

"Keep breathing to the count and I'll tell you,"

said the doctor as he lifted Mark's backpack off the chair and sat down.

"It was at Tabriz, in Iran—what they used to call Persia. I was with your dad there. When I was a boy, I heard about this young Venetian who went to China on the Road of Silk—'the road of all roads'—five thousand miles from the Mediterranean to China's Yellow River. A thousand years before Christ, rats, fireworks, oranges, silk, salt, slaves, and pepper were moving westward along that road."

Mark's eyes widened. "Rats?" he asked.

"Rats, umbrellas, noodles, hissing cockroaches, ideas, walnuts, opium, gunpowder, and a whole lot more.

"I found myself on it," Hornaday continued. "I saw men in headscarves, women in the black *hijab* that covered their faces. I ate figs and dates and grilled goat; I heard camel bells and drivers' calls and smelled the animals and the dung fires at night. The stars looked the way Marco Polo had described them."

Mark sat up so suddenly he started coughing again. "Dad gave me his book," he wheezed. "He's on the desert where Marco was on his trip. We haven't heard from him for a long time. We came here to find him. He's living with the herders, writing about them."

"Your father always was a brave man," said

Hornaday, gently pushing Mark down. "But take it easy. You don't want to get started hacking again."

Mark lay back. He was excited. He wondered how much Doc knew about the place where his dad was.

"What's so special about Marco Polo?" the doctor asked. "There were merchants and monks who went to the East before he did. They left reports, but nobody reads them. Why do we read Marco?"

The dog turned to watch Mark's face as if he was following the conversation.

"I don't know," Mark said, "but he sounds like he's the first one, like he's going into outer space. But Dad told me about some guy who tried to follow Polo's route from his book and got lost. Did Marco tell the truth?"

Hornaday nodded. "I'm pretty sure he went to Mongolia and China, and later to India. His last adventure is as full of truth as anything I've ever read—his coming-home story."

Mark nodded. "Mom and I went to where his house was," he said. "I went through the arch they walked under. That's all that's left."

Hornaday got up and took a spoon and a bottle of red liquid from his case. He shook the bottle and poured. "Swallow," he said, aiming the spoon.

"Argh!" the boy sputtered, spitting and making a face. "That's awful—like something you'd put in a car."

"Right," said Hornaday. "Pipe cleaner. Label says it's cherry-flavored."

"Don't believe it."

Doc shrugged. "Probably no worse than what the medicine man gave Marco when he got sick in the mountains."

"I haven't got to that part," Mark said. He looked hard at the doctor. "Can you tell me about Marco Polo?"

"Nobody knows much," Hornaday replied as he sat down again. "We know what's in his book, but beyond that? We don't even know what he looked like."

"I've seen pictures," Mark said. "The museum—"

The doctor cut him off. "Venice is full of Marco pictures—paintings and drawings, sculptures too—all done after he was dead. They didn't think much of him when he was alive, so they didn't paint and sculpt him like they did the priests and politicians we don't hear about anymore. Was he fair or dark? By some accounts, he had African blood, so maybe he looked like me. More than anything, though, I'd like to know who made him so curious about the East."

"Maybe his teacher at school?" Mark ventured. "Or his father and mother?"

Boss grew more and more restless, rattling his collar, sneezing, snorting, making a sort of humming noise.

"Does he need to go out?" Mark asked.

"Him? No," said Hornaday, reaching down and rubbing the dog's head. "Marco talk always gets him stirred up."

"How come?"

"He's got a family connection to Marco Polo's dog," the doctor explained.

Mark looked at Boss.

The dog grunted deeply.

"It wasn't Marco's parents that taught him about the East," Doc said. "His mother died soon after he was born, and his father left on a trading trip before he was three. Marco didn't see him again until he was fifteen. It must have been somebody else."

"Who then?" Mark asked.

"Nobody knows for sure. You'll just have to imagine it."

"You can't imagine history!" Mark exclaimed. "That's for stories."

"Really? Why?" the doctor asked. "History *is* stories. It comes from what the historian imagines. He soaks up everything he can and then imagines what happened. I bet if you pretend you're on your own like Marco was, you'll learn a lot," said Hornaday.

Boss thumped his tail.

"My dad's on his own like Marco," Mark said slowly. "Right now the people who sent him can't find him because the water dried up where he was supposed to be and he had to go somewhere else.

"Can you tell me about Marco's father?" Mark asked.

"He was a trader," the doctor began, "off with his brother on the Silk Road, swaying at the caravan's pace on one of the strands that ran to China and back, loaded down with the goods they'd taken on at Venice, poking their noses out like hungry squirrels, venturing farther and farther east to get the best price.

"They got caught between warring tribes. They were surrounded by a horde of horse warriors dressed in black."

Mark shivered. *What if that's what's happened to Dad?*

"How did they escape?" Mark asked.

"They didn't," said Hornaday. "The chief decided to take them to his cousin, Kublai Khan, conqueror of all China, emperor of the East. He figured Kublai would give him more for a pair of European slaves than he'd ever get for the captives' clothing and kit.

Marco's father and uncle ended up in Mongolia at Kublai's summer palace. They were the first Europeans he ever met—'Colored-Eye People,' he called them. Mongol eyes are black.

"Kublai was curious about Europe, so he sent them home with gifts for the doge—the Venetians' ruler—and a letter to the pope asking for a hundred teachers."

Mark's breathing was still ragged, but right now he wasn't thinking about how he felt.

"Did his father send letters home about what the East was like?" he asked.

"I don't think so," the doctor replied. "There wasn't any mail in those days. Maybe he tried to send back word with one of the caravans heading west, but I don't think Marco heard from him until he got back to Venice."

"Did he miss his dad?" Mark asked.

"I guess at first," the doctor said, "but as the years went by he must have come to think he was an orphan. It must mean something that he doesn't say much about him in *The Travels.*"

"Yeah, I guess," Mark said. "Did he read books about China while his dad was away?"

The doctor shook his head. "Marco lived before people in the West knew about printing," he said. "In his time books were handwritten on specially prepared sheepskins called parchment. They were so valuable they were kept on chains in the libraries. But I don't think Marco was a reader. Not many people were back then. Maybe he could read the merchants' manuals, but not much beyond that. How about you," Doc asked, "are you a reader?"

"Some," Mark said.

Hornaday rubbed the dog's ears.

"So nobody at home in Marco's time knew what China was really like?" Mark asked.

"The pope and the doge probably had some idea," Hornaday said, "but what they knew was really limited. Until Marco described it, few people in the West had any idea of China's immensity and variety of life. You know the story of the three blind men describing the elephant?" the doctor asked.

"Sure," said Mark. "One guy says it's like a long hose, the next guy says it's like the trunk of a tree, the third guy says it's like the side of a hairy ship."

"Right," said Hornaday. "Well, the returning missionaries and merchants were like those blind men, bringing back reports about the tiny parts they'd visited, totally ignorant of the whole."

Mark pushed himself back up on an elbow. "So you think until his father got back and told him about it, Marco didn't know anything about where he'd been?"

The doctor raised his eyebrows.

"He was fifteen when his father returned. By then I think he knew a lot."

"How? Who taught him?" Mark asked.

"He'd studied in the school of the street."

"What's *that*?"

As Hornaday drew the creaking chair up close, Boss twitched his tags.

"In any town that's where you'll find the best gossip, the biggest lies, and the truest truths," the doctor said. "Marco's Venice was a special place. Its school of the street was like no other in the world. Venice in those days was Europe's main port for goods from North Africa and the East. Every day the long black galleys arrived from Alexandria, Constantinople, Trebizond, and Acre, loaded with rare merchandise, slaves, sailors, and soldiers.

"Outside her taverns and alongside her docks and warehouses, old sailors lounged along with released slaves, worn-out pirates, and broken-down soldiers ending their days in sun-warmed corners. They'd traveled, they had tales, and Marco, being a boy, had ears. I think they taught him."

"How come he wasn't in regular school?"

Hornaday shook his head. "You're reading his book. Do you picture him sitting at a desk?"

Mark thought and then shook his head. "No. . . ."

"Me neither," said the doctor. "I see him slipping away to listen to men who knew things his teachers, the doge's spies, and the pope's missionaries had no idea of. Maybe the men of the street could tell him something about where his father was. That's what he was after: news of his father."

Just like me, Mark thought.

The doctor half closed his eyes as if he were squinting at something far away.

"I see Marco squatting in the warm sun, listening as an old man grows young telling what he's seen and heard, teaching an eager-faced boy the Ladino names of things he'd need on the Silk Road, telling him how to make his way in strange eastern places."

"What's Ladino?" Mark asked.

"One of the traders' languages," the doctor replied. "It's a blend of Spanish and Hebrew. It was a code that only a few people knew, so the traders could exchange secrets with each other without being understood by spies, servants, and ears behind the tent flaps."

Hornaday yawned.

"Imagine yourself as Marco, bored and curious, hanging around footloose on the docks, wondering where your father is. Close your eyes; maybe you'll meet his street teacher."

Pretty soon the doctor closed his own eyes. His breathing grew deep and steady with an occasional snore.

Mark fit the Chinese pillow under his head. Once he warmed it and moved it around a little, he began to get used to it. He closed his eyes. It wasn't very long before he saw a boy sitting on a broken crate beside a stranger on a stone-paved quay. The stranger's eyes were milky, almost unseeing. He was the color of old wood. There was the slap and smell of dark green seawater. The stranger shook open a large square of white cloth and wiped his watering eyes, then his face. There was the scent of oranges.

The boy had a sack of dried fruit. He held it out to the stranger, brushing the man's hands with it.

"Frutta," the boy said.

The man reached, then took.

"Grazie," the stranger rumbled. "You share with a beggar?" he asked, staring hard at the boy. His voice was hoarse, his accent strange.

"No, sir," the boy replied. "I take you for a traveler. Maybe you can tell me where my father is."

"He is a sailor, merchant, soldier, what?"

"A merchant. A trader."

The man nodded, pressing his large lips together. "And he set out for?"

"I don't know. The last we heard he was leaving Constantinople," said the boy.

"To come home?" the stranger asked.

"To go east," the boy answered.

"Ah," said the stranger as he dug in the sack. He didn't say anything more.

"Who are you?" the boy asked finally.

"A weary, almost blind old man," the stranger

answered. "I have nothing for you. Why do you bother with me?"

"For what you can tell me," the boy said.

For a long moment the dark man rocked silently from side to side like the sea marker in the channel beyond.

"Call me Mustafa," he said at last. "My name in my tribe is too long for you to remember. My people were Arabs of the desert, tent dwellers in the black tents of my tribe. We kept sheep and goats. When I was your age, a band of Tartars swooped out of a dry fog they'd conjured up with a devilish trick and captured my family. I was sold with our animals to a Silk Road caravan boss to help manage the beasts. At night by the fires I heard stories. Then I traveled the eastern road myself.

"The way of it is this," Mustafa continued. "To go where your father has gone, you must sail through pirate waters to where the desert begins. Once there you will head northeast, following the sunrising and the way of the Greek Wind. You will cross the broad plains and sand wastes where tribes of bandits like the men who captured me wait for you. They are thick-faced, those ones, with squashed noses and squat bodies. They will kill for a taste of butter or a pinch of salt.

"You will trust no one, least of all the oasis men,

for woe to the man that fainting or lingering falls into their hands. They will cut his throat for his purse. On the desert all look through their fingers and take nothing for the way it first appears."

"Ooh!" exclaimed the boy, his eyes wide.

"You are surprised?" asked the old Arab. "Listen, boy, men on the desert are wolves to each other. So what if they are hyenas to strangers? Distress of that place edges all men's spirits. They are reckless in the desert, cruel, greedy for anything of life. They have no souls. The heat, the cold, the burning light of that place kills all soul.

"Bribing or escaping those who would make a slave of you, you will go up mountains so steep that your horse must drag you as you hang on his tail. Then you will cross the unmarked desert where there is no water and as many die of cold as of heat.

"Now I teach you how to behave before the ruler of the East," the man said.

"Do you think I'll go there someday?" the boy asked.

The old Arab whispered, "Already you are on your way, boy. Listen," he rasped, "when you meet the great Kublai Khan, you will act like the proud European you are. You may bow a little, but you must not perform the Oriental greeting of submission, the forehead-to-floor *kowtow.*"

"Why not?"

"To surprise him. Do the unexpected. You must keep him unsure of what you are, your place in your tribe. Perhaps you are a prince? Do not show too much respect. Act bold as if you expect respect from him!

"It is said, boy, that in all the lands that Mongols rule not a dog might bark without his leave—but you, you must be different.

"If you put your neck down like one of his common subjects, the Oriental prince will step on it! Better you hold your head up. At worst he cuts it off; at best he takes you for what you are: fearless. Every day risk all. Hold nothing back and you may survive. Gather small gifts as you go: he is a child for presents. Glass beads from this place are as jewels to those people.

"Go now. Stand tall and think well of yourself. It will show. Act proud and even the emperor of the East will think the better of you. What he wants most to know is how the princes of Europe maintain their dignity. You will show him."

Mustafa paused and spat out an apricot pit.

He looked hard at the boy through his bleared

eyes. "Not all who set out on the Road of Silk return," he said.

He closed his eyes and sagged back against the mooring post.

After a pause the boy asked, "Will I see you again?"

"*Inshallah*—if it is the will of Allah," whispered the old Arab. "For now, farewell."

6

Boss Speaks Up

The room was quiet save for the sound of the doctor's deep breathing and occasional snores.

Then Boss rattled his tags.

Mark jerked up and looked around.

"Okay if I come up?" the dog whispered. "It's cold down here."

The dog was wagging his tail. Dried out, it was a big black plume.

Mark gasped.

"Boss?" he whispered. "You . . . you talk?"

The dog grumped and nodded.

"Up?" he asked again.

Mark patted the covers.

Boss glided up. Mark put his arm around him, curling his fingers in the dog's deep fur. It felt good. He liked the smell. It didn't make him sneeze.

"I wasn't really cold," Boss rumbled as he snuggled close. "I just said that so you'd let me up. My breed is from Tibet. It's cold there in the mountains, and we sleep outside, which is why my coat is so heavy. It sheds wet too. Except when I fall in the canal."

"Ooh!" Mark exclaimed, hugging the dog as if to save him. "Do you fall in a lot?"

"Once," Boss said with a shudder. "That was enough.

"It was a couple of years ago. I was a puppy. I stumbled getting off a pitching boat and got crushed between it and the dock. My master fished me out of the water, but I was a mess, leg broken, bleeding all over. He figured I was as good as dead, so he chucked me onto a passing garbage scow.

"Hornaday saw it happen. He flagged the scow, jumped aboard, waded through all the slime and stink, and picked me up. Filthy and bleeding as I was, he carried me close against his body.

"He took me to his office, laid me out on the table, and gave me a shot. I went numb. He washed me with doctor soap. It smells like chemicals. One sniff of it now and it all comes back. He painted my cuts with medicine so bitter I gave up trying to lick it off when the cuts started itching.

"It wasn't until he started to stitch my cuts that I

noticed his hands. He got hurt in Iraq trying to doctor a teacher at a girls' school when an unexploded bomb went off. He has to hold his right hand with his left to steady it.

"To cast my leg he made splints from kindling wood, snapping them to size on the table edge. The snaps sounded like when my leg broke.

"He put both hands on my chest. They were warm and dry, but they twitched. 'Easy now,' he said, looking me in the eye. 'Don't move.' His eyes are the color of chocolate, steady as dogs' eyes. His sweat has a sweet, strange smell. It's the medicine he takes for his twitch that makes him smell the way he does, but I didn't learn that until later.

"He began pulling and twisting my leg to line up the ends of bone. It didn't hurt, but I could feel the ends grinding together. It was like when you get dirt in your food and you chew it—you get this sandy grating sound in your head."

"Oh man," Mark groaned.

Boss grunted. "It was bad, all right. Doc said he should shave my leg before he taped it so the hair wouldn't pull when the break healed and he'd have to pull off the splints and everything, but he didn't have clippers, so he taped right over the hair.

"When he finished, my leg looked like a wrapped ham. When the break healed and he unwrapped me, it was like you stuck a piece of duct tape on your arm and then ripped it off—get it?"

Mark winced. "Yeah."

"The hair never did grow back right," Boss said, sticking out a motley-looking leg. The hair was wispy like the back of an old man's head.

"Doc told me I was lucky the bone had snapped clean," the dog said as he snuggled up against the boy again. "He said if it had been crushed, he would have had to put me down."

"Oh no!" Mark exclaimed so loudly he and Boss both looked to see if he'd awakened the doctor.

Suddenly the dog's blunt nose began twitching. "Have you got food up here?"

"Food?" the boy asked.

"Yes," said Boss, snuffling around. "I smell food."

"In my backpack at the foot of the bed—I've got some leftover frittata from breakfast. You want it?"

"Sure! I follow my mother's rule: Never pass up anything that smells good."

Mark reached into the backpack. He'd left it unzipped.

The napkin was empty. Not even a crumb.

"That's funny . . . ," he said.

"No, it isn't," Boss growled. "It's the rats. Turn your back, they steal."

"Rats up here?" Mark shuddered.

"They're everywhere," Boss whispered as he slipped lightly off the bed. "You find people, you'll find rats."

The dog nosed around.

"Let's see where they're getting in.

"Yup," he grunted. "There it is. See that crack there in the corner? That's his door. I'll bet his people have been working this place since Marco's time."

Mark got out of bed and looked at the crack.

"It's too small for a rat," he whispered.

"Uh-uh," muttered the dog. "Lemme tell you, to get at food rats can squeeze down like you wouldn't believe."

Boss squatted down in front of the crack. "Rat?" he called softly. "Rat? Come out."

There was a rustling, but no one came out.

"Never mind," said Boss. "He's embarrassed. Bring more frittata tomorrow, you'll meet him."

"I don't want to meet him. I want to put down poison."

"No," said Boss. "You don't want to do that. Rats have to live too."

"He'll bite me while I'm sleeping."

"I never heard that. You ever see anyone bit by a rat?"

"No . . . ," Mark said slowly.

"Me neither," said Boss. "Anyway, I heard you and Doc talking about Marco Polo. I know a lot about him."

"You?" exclaimed Mark.

"Hey," said Boss, sitting up and puffing out his chest, "a lot of what the doctor knows he got from me. My line goes back to the dog Marco met when he got sick in the mountains on his way to meet the great Kublai."

"The big black dog he returned to Venice with?" Mark said.

"That's my ancestor," said Boss. "His dog saved his life the night he came home, but that was years and years after Marco sat on the dock with Mustafa. You met Mustafa, right?" the dog asked.

Mark hesitated, then nodded.

"You want to know about Marco Polo?" Boss asked.

Mark nodded quickly and got beneath the covers again.

"I can tell you about him," Boss said, nodding his big head. "I got it from my great-great way back. He was with Marco for nearly everything that happened from the time the boy got sick in the mountains to his going to Kublai, his travels in China, and finally his trip back to Venice. He was along for all of it.

"And listen," said Boss in his deepest whisper, "if my forebear hadn't been with Marco the night they got back to Venice, you'd never have heard of Marco Polo, and neither would anybody else. So if you want to know about him, the place to start is the night of his homecoming."

Mark made a doubtful face.

Boss stiffened.

"Do you think I'm making it up?" he huffed.

"No, no," Mark whispered.

"The story was passed down to me," Boss said importantly. "Dogs have history just like people. We know. We remember. We don't start fresh, generation after generation, dumb as the first jackal that hung around a caveman hoping for a bone.

"Listen," whispered Boss, nudging Mark's head with his wet nose and giving him a lick. "Are you really awake? If you are, I'll tell you what Marco's homecoming was really like."

"I'm awake," the boy whispered, twisting away from the dog's nose as he wiped his face.

Just then something moving on the floor caught Mark's eye. The boy peered hard at the corner. There

was a small gray figure rocking on its haunches.

"We're awake too," the figure said. "We'll keep Boss straight. We were there too, you know."

"Jeez!" Mark shuddered, snatching up the covers. "Rats!"

Now there were five pairs of glittering dot eyes.

Boss laughed. "I told you he'd show," he said. "Rats can't pass up a story any more than they can pass up frittata. That's Count Leonardo and his clan.

"It's true what Leo says," Boss added. "His kind were around the night Marco came home."

"We were around here a long time before that," Leo boasted. "We came in on the first boats."

Mark leaned up on an elbow.

"Do you bite people?" he whispered.

"Do you?" asked the rat.

7

Marco's Homecoming

Mark pulled the quilt up to his chin. He was uneasy about the rats being so close.

"Okay," whispered Boss in his husky, rumbling voice. He kept it low so as not to awaken the doctor.

"When Marco left Venice with his father and uncle, they expected to be gone four or five years. They were gone more than twenty. People thought they were dead. In those days if no one heard from you or got word about you for a long time like that, your name got entered in a book and your property was given away.

"Put yourself in Marco's place. Imagine leaving home today and not returning for twenty-four years! You'd look different. Everyone you saw would look different, and they'd only remember you the way you'd looked the last time they'd set eyes on you.

What would you say? How would you identify yourself?"

"I don't know," Mark murmured. He felt the anxiety of it in the pit of his stomach. He realized he had no way of proving who he was. If you're not recognized in a place, who are you? Where do you belong?

"What would you do?" the dog asked. "Nobody knows you. Nobody has reason to trust you. You're at the mercy of others. Maybe they're scared of you just because of the way you look. I know about that! You saw how it was—that clerk out there would have kicked me down the stairs if he could have."

"Which you would have deserved, coming in here stinking and muddy, shaking your dog wet all over," Count Leo scolded. "But as for looks scaring folks off, the boy beside you shivers just looking at us rats."

"Silenzio!" Boss growled.

"What would you do?" he asked Mark again. "You've come home and nobody recognizes you. What's so special about you that you could use to get people to remember who you are?"

"There's nothing special about me," Mark whispered, shaking his head. "I guess I'd ask if they remembered the boy who couldn't breathe."

"That's it!" the dog exclaimed. "That's exactly how Marco proved who he was."

"What happened?"

"We'll get there," Boss said. "Right now it's dark and silent at Ca Polo, just after midnight on a moonless foggy night. These three tough-looking guys show up with this big dog at the family palazzo: Marco, his uncle and father, and my great-great. Marco looked nothing like the boy he'd been. The Polos looked like greasy beggars, hair oiled and tied back under filthy turbans, skins stained an odd color from the grease and juices they'd rubbed on for disguise and protection against the desert sun. Their boots were wolf-skin galoshes with the hair inside."

Boss's ruff was up. "They looked like bandits or worse," he said. "They'd been gone so long they'd forgotten Venetian manners. Even their speech was strange with Persian and Mongol thrown in. Like Mongols, they spat every time they finished speaking. They smelled."

"Spat?" Mark interrupted. "They spat when they talked?"

"Listen," Boss whispered, "that was the least of it. Their personal habits would have shamed a rat."

"Maybe even a dog," the count hissed.

Boss acted as if he hadn't heard. "They crowded under the entry arch," he continued, "three men, a gray donkey, and the great Tibetan dog—the biggest dog ever seen in Venice—my great-great generations back. He's the hero here."

Mark sat up. "I know that arch," he whispered. "I saw it earlier today. I stood under it."

Boss nodded. "It was a dangerous time. Venice was at war with Genoa. Spies lurked. The place was full of secrets and enemies. Every stranger looked suspicious. Were these guys thugs? The only baggage they had was what was on the back of Marco's donkey. Their stuff from China was still on shipboard. They had no papers. Who were they? They had no keys. They were locked out."

Hornaday erupted in a loud snore. Boss froze. The doctor shifted in the creaking chair, there was another rumble, then the rhythm of sleep again.

"The donkey was tired and hungry," Boss whispered. "He twitched his huge ears and tossed his harness bells. He could smell the other animals and their food. He stomped and shifted as he waited for the door to open. His load was heavy; the straps chafed.

"His master pulled at the bell rope and called out, 'I'm Marco Polo, let me in!'

"Nothing happened.

"My forebear cocked his head and looked at his master. He was used to seeing people jump and shout *'Obbedisco!'*—I obey—when Marco ordered. But no!

More tugs on the bell cord, more yells. The door stayed barred.

"The donkey began to bray for help. A donkey's cry is awful to hear, a whine as it winds up, then a hoarse scream like an engine breaking apart.

"This donkey's cry was desperate. The animals inside heard and understood. The roosters squalled, house dogs barked, the goats, sheep, horses, and donkeys all joined in, kicking at their stalls. Neighbors opened their shutters and looked out. *'Che cosa?'* they yelled. 'What's going on?' The town watchmen came with their lanterns.

"My great-great was panting now, standing with his paws apart, teeth showing. His paws were huge," Boss said, lifting up one of his.

" 'Who are you?' the watchmen demanded, crowding forward with their lamps. 'What are you doing here? Go away or we will jail you for disturbing the peace!'

"The dog rumbled. The watchmen edged back.

"The donkey brayed on, louder and louder, 'I am fainting! I am dying! Help me!'

"Suddenly a curious stable boy pushed the side door open a crack to see what was going on.

"The donkey charged in, knocking the boy down. Marco and the others followed into the stable and warehouse that was the first floor of Casa Polo.

“By now the whole house was up. Torches flared as men and women in nightshirts stood yelling from the balcony, waving open blades and knobbed clubs. The Polos held up their hands to show they had no weapons.

"They had the dog, though, and, if I do say so myself, he was magnificent. He looked huge, his ruff up, teeth showing. Nobody came near as he stood beside his master."

Boss's ruff was up all the way now, his big tail switching like a heavy rope.

"'Listen!' cried Marco. 'I am Marco Polo, one of your people. Where is my aunt? If she doesn't recognize my father, she will know me by this scar,' he said, pushing back his hair to show a dent in his left temple. 'I fell down those stairs and slashed my head on the corner of that chest. Does no one remember? Where is my aunt?'

"'She was a big, laughing, black-haired woman. She had a white line here on her lip, where it turned up from a fall she took—does no one remember? Where is she?'

"No one answered. They didn't want to believe the wild-looking strangers below were the missing Polos."

"Why?" Mark interrupted. "Weren't they glad to have their family back?"

"They thought it was a trick," Boss explained. "The Polos had been gone so long they were as good as dead. Their property had been given away. If those strangers really were the Polo men, the folks standing on the balcony would have to give everything back—

even the house they were living in—so they didn't want to believe Marco and his father and uncle had actually returned.

" 'The Polos were merchants,' growled the biggest man on the balcony. 'They had money when they left. Have you got money?'

" 'No,' said Marco. 'But I have the pass of gold that allowed us to travel through the lands of silk and spices at no charge and without injury. Surely if all those we passed coming here trusted and protected us on the strength of it, you should give us a chance to prove who we are!'

"With that, he drew from his coat a flat stick of gold marked with strange characters. It looked like what you'd stir a can of paint with.

" 'This is the *paiza* the Great Khan gave us when we left his city, Khanbaliq, the capital of all China,' Marco said. 'It lets everyone know we are guests of the emperor. The falcon seal at the top means we are his most preferred people.

" 'Here!' he said, tossing it up to the gravel-voiced man who seemed to be in charge.

"This man weighed it, bit it, then tossed it back.

" 'Fake!' he said with a sneer.

"He motioned to the others on the balcony. 'They're thieves!' he yelled. 'Drive them out!'

"My forebear inched toward the stairs, crouched low, his jaws slobbering.

"He did the slobbering for effect," Boss explained. "Our breed doesn't slobber."

The rats snickered.

"So why does the doctor have to wipe your face when you go into the signora's café?" Leo teased.

Boss drew himself up. "That's drooling, not slobbering. Never mind them," he said, turning to Mark. "Are you still with me?"

"Yes," Mark whispered.

"Good," said the dog. "As the men started down the stairs, my great-great lunged at them, snarling and snapping, shredding the leader's nightshirt with a swipe of his paw.

"There were screams and stumbling. The men retreated.

"Then silence.

"In that instant Marco remembered the identifying thing that *you* mentioned: Marco, too, once had trouble breathing.

" 'My nurse!' he shouted. 'She was famous in our family for saving my life when I gagged on gristle and turned blue. She was old and weak, but she shoved me to the floor and then hoisted me up feetfirst and pounded my back until I coughed out the piece that was choking me.

" 'The neighbors all heard the story. The priest told it in church as a miracle. Surely you remember me now!' he cried. 'I'm the boy who was choking and couldn't breathe.'

"Slowly the oldest house servants began to nod. 'Yes,' said one, 'that must be Marco, and that *vecchio*—that old one—his uncle, and that one, there, his father.'

"The deep-voiced man on the balcony—the guy in the ripped nightshirt who was going to clobber the intruders—puckered up his face. His eyes began to water.

"Slowly he lowered his club.

" '*Miracolo! Miracolo!*—Miracle! Miracle!' he whispered. 'Welcome home!'

"He was Marco's cousin, the one who had inherited the most and now would have to give it all up.

" 'A feast!' he ordered.

"He and Marco had played together as children in the campo out front. They had rowed in the regatta together and teased the neighbor girls. He remembered now. He smiled through tears. The two men embraced.

" 'Food!' the others called. 'Wine!'

"'My dog and my donkey!' Marco said. 'First I see to them.'

"With his own hand Marco fed his dog chunks of cold veal from the kitchen. The donkey got fresh green hay and grain with salt and honey. Marco hugged his animals for a long moment, then kissed them. 'But for you two,' he whispered, 'we'd still be in the alley.'"

Boss sat up. He towered over Mark.

"So now you see how it was," he whispered. "But for my great-great's bravery that night, those people would have murdered Marco.

"When you think about it, they had every reason to. First this rough-looking guy busts into their fortress, then he claims to be its true owner. What would you do? The dog saved them."

Boss went on: "If my forebear hadn't helped Marco get inside that house and—risking his own neck—held off those people long enough for Marco to prove who he was, no one would ever have heard of Marco Polo or his travels, and there'd never have been that book."

The dog paused and shook himself. It felt like an earthquake on the bed.

Boss looked over at the rats. Their tails were switching as one.

"Okay so far," said Count Leo. "Hurry up! Go on!"

Boss took a deep breath and began again. "Only when the first birds called did the household go to sleep," he said. "That's when Marco almost lost everything."

8

Marco Goes Crazy

"It was three in the morning," said Boss, "maybe four, and all these Polos and Ca Polo people were drinking and eating and telling stories and interrupting each other and laughing and banging the table.

"At last the travelers staggered upstairs and fell into bed. The sun rose.

"And then it happened—but you know what happened," the dog said, stopping suddenly and looking hard at Mark.

"No, I don't. Tell me. Please," Mark whispered.

"You don't remember what happened when Marco woke up?" the dog asked, pushing his big face so close to Mark's the boy could feel his hot breath. "You didn't read it in Marco's book?"

"I—I didn't get that far," Mark stammered. "Could you tell me the story? I see better when I'm listening."

"So do we," chorused the rats.

The dog rearranged himself carefully into his Sphinx-like storytelling posture: head up, front paws out straight, rears tucked under, big plume tail curled around.

"Venetians have always been proud of their clothing," he said. "Marco's traveling coat was worn and stinking, not worth saving, so a servant girl had been ordered to give it to a beggar who'd come to the door.

"When Marco woke up and reached for his coat, he panicked. He searched and yelled until he learned what the girl had done. He whispered to his father, then stuffed something inside his shirt and dashed out of the house.

"Dressed in what remained of his Tartar costume, he raced across the campo with my great-great galloping beside him. Folks jumped out of the way when they saw that pair coming! Together they crossed the humped bridge over the little canal that served as the family lane and hurried to the Rialto Bridge—the most important bridge in Venice."

"I've seen it!" Mark exclaimed. "Mom took me there yesterday."

"Good, so you've got the setting for the gambit."

"Gambit?" Mark asked. "What's a gambit?"

"Uh . . ." Boss hesitated.

"It's from the Italian word for tripping someone," the old rat yelled.

"Right," said Boss. "I knew; I was just testing them.

"In Marco's time," he continued, "the Rialto Bridge was made of wood. It was a big white arch without steps so mules and horses could get over, and tall enough so the biggest galleys could pass underneath. The sides were open so folks could see out, and there was a flat space at the top where people could catch their breath and gossip. A walker looking down could see everything passing on the canal; a boatman looking up could see who was there.

"Marco searched the crowd as he rushed up the steps. When he got to the top, he reached into his shirt and took out a red and yellow pinwheel made of stiffened paper and marked with strange characters painted in black. My great-great stood panting at his side."

Boss was panting now.

"People rushed past," he said. "At first they ignored Marco, but then one old merchant slowed and stared, then another and another until a crowd stood blocking the bridge, watching, as this odd-looking, greasy-haired man with the giant dog wove and staggered, holding his pinwheel.

"Marco kept looking around, his eyes bugged out

like he was scared to death, his mouth gaping, spit dripping out. Nobody got too close—he might be a madman, any moment jumping on someone, scratching and biting. It had happened. People gawked. 'Who are you?' they called. 'What are you doing?'

"'He will come if God pleases,' Marco said in his odd half-Venetian, half-Mongol speech.

"He wouldn't say more. Maybe he couldn't. He stood there pitching like a moored boat in wind, aiming his pinwheel into the breeze. He struggled to keep his face smooth. 'Serene like the Buddha,' he told himself as he chanted what he'd heard the monks in China mumble before their huge temple figures.

"'Serene like the Buddha,' he reminded himself when his stomach lurched. 'Serene like the Buddha,' but his heart was pounding and his body shook. He had to get that coat back.

"He felt dizzy as he looked around. Venice had been his home once—the rich center of the world. Now it seemed small. It *was* small compared to the capital of China, where he'd just been.

"For years he'd dreamed about coming home, imagined and hoped for it more than anything. Now he wondered if he'd made a mistake. And to have lost his coat!

"For two days and nights Marco stood on top of the Rialto Bridge, fixed in place like one of those men you see in the squares posing like statues, only Marco wasn't posing. He was cold and wet and pale, weaving like a man in a trance as he held his pinwheel in the wind.

"His father came with food. He begged his son to quit. There was a rumor that the doge and his council were talking about arresting Marco for being a nuisance on the Rialto.

"Marco pretended not to hear his father.

"An old friar took pity and brought him cups of wine and crusts of bread."

Mark was sitting up straight and staring. "Did Marco stand outside all night," he whispered, "in the fog and cold and everything? And why was he holding the pinwheel?"

"All night," Boss said softly, "and all day the next day and all the following night. The pinwheel was to get attention—no one in Venice had ever seen one—to get people to come, as many as possible, so maybe he'd spot his coat in the crowd."

"Wow!" Mark murmured.

Just then the doctor snorted again.

They all jumped—Mark, Boss, and the rats—but the doctor slept on.

"Quick!" the old rat whispered excitedly. "Get on with it!"

"The passers-by all stared hard at Marco," Boss said. "They would have poked him with a stick to get him to talk, but they kept their distance because of the dog. They were afraid of him. One child, though, was not afraid. She brought bread and milk and petted him. She wasn't afraid. It's only when people get older that they learn fear.

"Word spread all over Venice. Street kids came in gangs to taunt Marco. *'Il pazzo,'* they jeered—'touched in the head.'

"On the morning of the third day, Marco recognized his old coat on a man who'd come to see the fool with the giant dog and the pinwheel.

"Marco pretended to be drunk. He staggered toward the stranger, making strange gurgling noises and waving the whirligig so hard it began to shred. He was acting so scary and peculiar even his dog hung back.

" 'My friend! My friend!' Marco yelped, embracing the man. 'I am freezing. *Freezing!* Sell me your coat. Look, I give you all my money,' he said, turning out his pockets.

"When Marco bought back his shabby coat for his last coins—a sum equal to what a dockworker earned in a week—the crowd figured he was a greater fool yet.

"He put on the coat. Then he put his hands together and bowed deep in the Buddhist manner to the four winds.

"When he returned to Ca Polo, he called for a blade and asked everyone to sit down as he took off the mess of rags he'd just paid so much for.

"His people looked at him the way the crowds on the Rialto had.

"Nodding and smiling as he muttered to himself, he slit seam after seam, pulling apart tufts of filthy wool stuffing to reveal a fortune in pearls, emeralds, sapphires, diamonds, coral, topazes, turquoise, and rubies. There was even a strange seashell in his treasure, a white cowrie shell that had served for money in India.

"No one ever calculated how much treasure Marco came home with. Rumor made it huge—huger than it really was, judging from how plainly he lived later on.

"His stories were what people talked about. He told of the measureless immensity of China—a land vaster and with greater ports and canals and everything bigger than anything any Venetian had ever seen or heard tell of, of spike-shaped jade green mountains split by swift rivers more than a mile across, and of huge armies that could make the sky dark at midday with stinking smokes, flashes of lightning and blasts of thun-

der to terrify their enemies—fireworks! He told of Kublai's palaces and his twelve thousand 'trusty ones' on horseback, of his knights in golden robes trimmed in crimson, of his four wives, each with ten thousand attendants, of the palace dance troupe of thirty thousand, of the one hundred thousand white camels and horses Kublai got for his birthday, of his fortune: 'Ducats in the millions!' Marco told about where he'd been, what he'd seen—places and things richer than anything anyone had ever heard of or seen, everything huger and grander than the fabulously wealthy Venetian Republic. He told about a great Chinese spice port one hundred miles around with twelve thousand bridges and twelve gates, each manned by a thousand guards. It was all too much for his neighbors. A port vaster than Venice? An empire greater than the Venetian? Rich cities no one had ever heard of? No. *'Impossibile!'* they whispered to one another.

"Hearing Marco go on in his odd way of speaking, his listeners thought maybe he was mocking them. After all, the Venetians were the world's great ones! Who were these rich Chinese he was babbling about? What kind of people kept pet crickets in ivory cages? What were goldfish?

"Even his old friends thought him a bragging fool, or worse. His stories about everything being so much and so many embarrassed them. At one gathering he told in a loud voice about a place 'where they dig black stones from the mountains, which burn and make flames like logs and keep up the fire and cook better than wood does. And these stones are so good that nothing else is burnt.' "

"Coal," Mark whispered.

Boss nodded. "No one in Venice knew about coal then.

"Marco's stories made him famous," the dog went on, "but not like you or I would like to be famous. He became a famous fool, a laughingstock. Some took to calling him *Marco Milione,* 'Marco of the Millions.' It started as a tease, and it stuck.

"Marco's nickname followed him all the rest of his life. Little children used to run after him calling, 'Marco Milione, tell us another lie.'

"Every morning he'd pass the place where he'd sat listening to Mustafa years before, half expecting to see his old Arab friend. It was empty now. Marco was an old man. Things were different. He was a figure of fun. Sure as anything, no kid would come sit to hear *his* story. Not that he could sit on a broken crate and spend the day taking in the sun and talking to children. That was for beggars.

"Mustafa had been comfortable sitting on his box. He'd been poor, but he'd been easy in his heart, proud that a young boy had come to him begging stories. That had made him feel rich. It was different for Marco."

"Liar! Liar! Pants on fire," Mark whispered.

Boss nodded. "But it was all true. What Marco told them was true. As he lay dying, the priest came. 'Clear your conscience, Marco,' he urged. 'Confess that you have lied.'

"Marco shook his head, 'I have not told the half of what I've seen,' he said as he turned to the wall.

"Those were his last words."

"Marco Milione," Mark whispered after a pause. "Did the nickname hurt his feelings?" he asked.

"Sure. Nicknames are meant to hurt," the dog replied. "Don't you have one?"

"Yeah. A boy at school calls me Question Mark."

Boss nodded. "So you understand. For me it's *Cavallo*—Horse—because of my size."

"Tell me about it," said Leo sadly. "Our family name *is* a nickname—*Ratto.* You want to slur somebody around here, call him Ratto."

It was quiet in the room. The only sound was the doctor's deep breathing, now and then broken with snores.

"Good job, Boss," whispered the count, rocking back and forth. "But you know that stuffing Marco pulled from his coat? The rats at Ca Polo saved it—good oily stuff with sheep grease and all the drips that had seeped in through a thousand meals—best bedding we've ever had, passed down from generation to generation. Sometimes when they're bored or hungry, the children suck on a wad to get the juice of those ancient dinners. When I go visit, I take a chaw myself. Tasty! We even found that strange white seashell you mentioned. Must have been Marco's good luck piece.

"Got to go now," said Leo. "Got to get to the signora's. Her garbage is the best. Deal is, she sorts it for us, so we stay outta her kitchen. Sweet lady. She knows how tough it is to scratch a living out of this wet place."

There was a skittering of small clawed feet, then silence.

Mark dozed off, only half hearing when Hornaday and Boss clomped down the sixty-eight stairs. Then silence. After a long time he heard the heavy front door clank shut.

Dad,

I got really sick and couldn't breathe like at home when you get up and give me hot water with lemon juice and whiskey, but this was worse and the medicine I got was worse. Mom got your army friend Dr. Hornaday to come. You wouldn't believe his dog. He's a giant and he can do things I'll have to tell you about when I see you because writing them you'd think I was crazy. Doc knows a lot about Marco Polo too—did you guys have to study him in the army? Doc says you're brave to be doing what you're doing. There's a store near the big bridge here that sells nothing but chess sets. I got you a really small one for Christmas so we can play together on trips. It won't add anything to your backpack. Mom says because there's no light at night where you are, nobody reads or plays chess. They sit around and sing really long songs that tell their history and they all know all the words. Is this what you're writing down? I hope you're OK. I hope we hear about you soon.

Your son, Mark

9

STEALING THE BONES

Mark was awake and writing his dad when his mother tapped at the door. He stuffed the red notebook under his pillow.

"How do you feel?" she asked, sticking her head in.

"Better," he answered.

"Good! Are you well enough to go over to the signora's for breakfast?"

Mark nodded. He was better, but he felt odd. His head buzzed with voices—Mustafa's, Boss's, Count Leo's. He wasn't sure whether what he'd seen and heard was some kind of a fever dream or had really happened.

Hornaday and Boss were waiting for them outside the café. The dog wagged and sang a high *humm* of welcome when he saw Mark.

The boy smiled and gave his new friend a pat.

They all went in together. There was a fresh rose on their table and music like yesterday, brisk and light.

Boss laid his head on Mark's foot. Surprised, the boy jerked his foot away. Boss found it again. His head was heavy and warm. Mark let it stay.

His mother ate quickly. "I want to get over to the agency," she said, "find out what I can, talk to those people, get some answers." She paused and looked at Mark. "Not much fun for you, though."

"That's okay," said Mark. "I'll go."

Hornaday leaned back in his chair. "If he likes, Mark can stay with me and Boss. If he's up for it, we could go looking for Marco together."

He turned to the boy. "That interest you?"

Mark nodded. "Yeah. Sure."

"Shouldn't he lie low after last night?" Mark's mother asked.

"Not one of my preferred remedies," Hornaday said as he reached into his case. "Boredom makes some things worse."

He turned to Mark. "Let's listen to you." He pressed the stethoscope against Mark's chest.

"Clearer," he said as he put the instrument back. "Not a hundred percent, but a whole lot better. He can manage a tour."

"That's nice of you, Doc," Mark's mother said.

"I'm not doing it to be nice," the doctor said. "Having Mark here gives me an excuse to poke around. I've read a lot about Marco Polo, but I've never gone looking for him."

Mark heard his father's voice in his head: *Sleuthing. Sleuthing beats sightseeing.*

"Okay, then!" his mom said brightly as she got up to leave.

"Wait, Mom," Mark said, pulling the red notebook from his pocket. He tore out some pages and folded them. "Give these to the agency guys for Dad, okay? He probably won't get them, but . . ."

"He'll get them!" she said firmly. She kissed Mark and hurried off.

Hornaday got out the red medicine.

"Aw no, Doc!" Mark protested. "I'm better enough without it."

"I bet it doesn't taste any worse than what Marco got when he was sick in the mountains," the doctor said. "His probably had snake gizzard and lizard liver in it."

"Next time lizard liver," Mark groaned.

"If Marco had gotten sick in Venice," Hornaday said as he shook the bottle, "he might have been given oil of red dog."

"What's *that*?" Mark asked.

Doc's eyes shone. "Just what it sounds like. A whole red dog—hair and all—was boiled in oil with ten scorpions and a lot of pepper. After a couple of hours the juice was strained off and the lucky patient got to drink it."

Boss moaned like a deep siren winding down.

"Ugh!" Mark exclaimed.

"Right," said Hornaday, "so here we go."

He aimed the spoon. His hand trembled.

Mark made a face and swallowed. "How come your hands shake?" the boy asked as he wiped his mouth.

"I've got a tic," the doctor said.

"A tick like a clock, back and forth?"

"No, not like that," said Hornaday. "It's nerve damage. The muscles move on their own. When I was in Iraq with your dad, we were trying to rescue a young woman, an American teacher who'd been gassed in the war. I inhaled some of the poison."

"What do you mean, gassed? Like air pollution?" Mark wanted to know.

"The enemy had dropped bombs that squirt a gas in the air that burns away soft tissue like lungs and destroys nerves," the doctor said. "I got some."

"Who was the enemy?" Mark asked. "What happened to the teacher?"

"Not now," said Hornaday, his face stiffening.

He waved to the signora. She nodded and came over. "So where do you look for Messer Milione today?" she asked Mark. "You have been to San Marco?"

"Not yet."

"Ah, there you must go," she said, putting out her arms as if she were handing him something. "It is our best church because of the law that every merchant had to bring back a beautiful for it. Your Marco went there on feast days."

"Does it still look like it did when Marco saw it?" he asked.

"Sì, sì, sì," the signora said. "The domes outside are the same, the apostles in gold inside—you look around, you see through Marco Polo eyes.

"But if there is a Mass," she cautioned, raising her hands, "wait. It is not long. It is not good for tourists to disturb."

"Let's go," the doctor said as he stood and wrapped his red scarf around his neck. "It's not far, just a loop along the Grand Canal."

Boss was up and shaking out his coat, his great tail swinging back and forth.

They set out, the doctor striding smooth and straight-backed. Eyeing him, Mark stood a little straighter and tried to match his stride. Boss limped along between them.

"What religion was Marco?" Mark asked.

"Catholic," the doctor replied. "That was the official church in Europe then, but I think he was more interested in learning about the religions he met than in telling folks about his own.

"He had the mind of a merchant, not a missionary, but the Buddhists he encountered in China—'idolators' he called them, but not in a sneering way—made a big impression. He mentions them often, and their temples."

"What religion are you?" Mark asked.

Hornaday shrugged. "I'm a doctor. Medicine takes in all religions. Illness doesn't choose among sects. Muslim, Catholic, Jew, Buddhist, Protestant, Hindu, pagan, atheist—the bodies are all the same."

"Okay," said Mark, "but what about when you were a kid?"

"A.M.E. African Methodist Episcopal."

"What church is that?"

"A church for black Protestants. In slavery time blacks weren't allowed in the white churches, so they organized their own.

"What religion are you?" Hornaday asked.

"Mom's a Lutheran, Dad's a Quaker," Mark said.

"We switch back and forth. With Quakers nobody's in charge—people just wait around until somebody gets up to say something. With Lutherans there's a program to show how close you are to the end of the service, so I like that better."

They stood aside for a struggling porter wheeling a handcart heavy with jugs of wine.

"Just like a thousand years ago," Hornaday said. "Everything you see has been floated in and moved by hand—all the paving stones, clothes, bricks, oil, food—all of it."

The vaporetto stop was a gently pitching barge tied up at an opening on the Grand Canal. Across the water the sun had caught the front of a church with gold ornaments and a palace with a covered porch on the top. There was a square and docks, but no grass in sight anywhere.

"Where do kids play?" Mark asked.

"In the streets, the campos, but mostly on the water. The sea is their playground. Venetian kids grow up swimming, rowing, and sailing. They have boat races year-round—regattas."

The waterbus arrived with a lot of engine noise, splashing and slithering. Its wake sent the dock heaving as the captain worked the big tan boat up against the stop. It was crowded, big as a street bus, dirty and rusted.

The dog hung back.

Hornaday took him by the collar. "Okay, boy," the doctor said as he led Boss up the heaving gangplank.

"He had a bad experience with a boat once," the doctor explained, "which is why we walk most everywhere."

Mark already knew.

Striped poles banded blue and red and green and yellow announced intersections. In the channel there

were speed signs just like on land: 5 MPH—but most of the boats were going faster than that. As they rode, Mark pointed to the sunstruck buildings. "Did Venice look like this when Marco was here?" he asked.

"If he came back today, he'd recognize it," the doctor said, "but it would look worn down, because there isn't enough money to keep things fixed up.

"In Marco's time Venice was rich beyond imagining. The Piazza San Marco, where we're headed, was home to the cathedral, but it was also the biggest and most famous marketplace in the Western world. All the goods of the East came through here because the port of Venice was closest to the heart of Europe. Everything was traded in the piazza—jewels, silk, slaves, spices, soap, perfumes, ivory, drugs. Every ship brought in the choicest goods from the caravans that had opened their bundles and bags where the Silk Road ended.

"Remember the signora saying how every merchant had to bring back something for the church? Well, much of it was booty, stuff plundered from Egypt, Greece, and Persia. Venetians looted everywhere they landed. They were called 'sea sharkers.'

"Their biggest haul came when Marco's father was a boy. The Venetians sacked Constantinople, then the richest Christian city in the world. The four great bronze horses you'll see out front, the columns inside—no two alike—most of the sculptures, all the marble, the gold in the dome of the apostles—it was all stolen."

Mark began walking fast when they got off the boat. He wanted to see the horses robbed from Constantinople. Doc made the church sound like a thieves' paradise with valuables piled up in the corners.

Boss picked up the boy's excitement. He lifted his nose as if he were scenting game.

"The wonder is what they made of what they took," Hornaday was saying. "Ancient stone columns, panels of veined marble—the builders and artists turned it into something holy. Some of the gold was melted and spread thin on tiny pieces of glass to make the ceiling mosaics. They did the same thing with the floor, cutting and fitting thousands of semiprecious stones into beautiful patterns."

Mark was walking faster and faster, his head filled with images of Venetian robbers staggering under sacks of treasure.

"Why did they have to steal stuff?" he asked, breathing hard. "You said Venice was really rich."

"She wasn't always," Hornaday said, putting out his hand to slow Mark a little. "That's why robbery figures so much in her history. She had a lot of catching up to do to become as grand as her rival, Genoa.

"Genoa was in her glory and Venice was nothing more than a cluster of huts when marauders came out of the north and sent people fleeing here.

"The newcomers looked around. 'What do we have to work with?' they wondered.

"They sold fish, made salt, melted sand to make glass, and they built boats. They were soon sailing out into the Adriatic and down to the Mediterranean as merchant raiders."

Mark looked out over the water as if he expected to catch sight of one.

"For all its elegance," the doctor was saying, "there's always been an air of stealth and thuggery about this place. It was never holy like Assisi or noble like Rome, but for the sake of their religion the Venetians pulled off their greatest heist when they stole the bones of the Apostle Mark."

"Stole his bones?" Mark exclaimed. "Why'd they do that?"

"Folks believed they'd bring good luck," Hornaday said. "Don't you carry something for luck?"

"Yeah," said Mark as he felt in his pocket for the flint scraper he'd found on a trip with his dad. He didn't know why, but he was sure it was lucky.

"The saint's remains were buried in Alexandria in Egypt," the doctor explained. "When Alexandria fell to the followers of Islam, it was rumored here in Venice that the sultan had ordered St. Mark's church pulled down and his bones thrown into the common garbage pit.

"Two young Venetian merchants worked themselves into a frenzy over this. 'Pitch the apostle's remains into the garbage pit?' they cried to each other. 'We must save him!'

"They set out in a borrowed boat. The pope had banned Christians from stopping in Muslim Alexandria, and the Egyptians weren't exactly welcoming, so the Venetians broke up some of the ship's rigging and limped into port, pretending to have been blown in by bad weather.

"There was a long exchange with the port officials about the ancient rule that harborage and courtesies had to be afforded distressed sailors. Finally, with the passing over of a bit of silver, the Venetians were allowed to dock.

"They went ashore and bought the tools they said they needed to fix their ship. Tools in hand, they sneaked over to St. Mark's church and bribed the old caretaker to let them in. Once inside they tied him up, barred the door, and set to work getting Mark's bones.

"This took some doing. His bones and hair and the cape and crown and shoes he'd been buried in weren't just sitting in a suitcase ready to go. It took hammers, crowbars, and chisels to tear down the altar and pry away masonry to get at the heavy stone box containing his body. They worked all night. Finally at dawn they cracked open Mark's sarcophagus. A sweet smell filled the church and the neighborhood around. Nobody knew what it was."

"Huh?" Mark asked. "Wouldn't old bones stink?"

Hornaday laughed. "Maybe they did, but the legend has it that they smelled good. Anyway," he continued, "the Venetians stuffed the saint's remains in the sack they'd carried their tools in and hurried to the dock, pretending to be carrying stuff to fix their ship. The fragrance they'd noticed in the church surrounded them—an odor so pleasing, the story goes, it was as if all the spices in Alexandria had been tossed into the air.

"Just as they got the bones on board, the sultan heard that people were rushing out of their homes, singing and dancing in the street, seemingly crazed by a miraculous sweet fragrance.

"He sent his soldiers to investigate. They couldn't smell the sweetness themselves, so they stumbled around for hours asking people what it was, where it was coming from.

"At last they discovered the tied-up watchman and the robbers' tools. The once-fine altar was rubble. The watchman told them what had happened. The soldiers hurried to the Venetians' ship.

"Meanwhile the robbers, knowing the Muslims' aversion to pork, had buried Mark's relics in a barrel of freshly salted pig meat and hung strips of pork around their ship, pretending to be curing provisions in the salt air while they fixed their rigging.

"When the sultan's agents got to the boat, they found the sight—and worse, the smell—of those bloody strips revolting.

"*'Hanzir! Hanzir!'* they screeched. 'Pork! Pork!' The tub of pink pig flesh under its veil of salt made them sick. They didn't stay to dig around in it; they fled, retching.

"The Venetians were under sail by the time the sultan's ship heaved anchor. The robbers were blown along by what seemed a divine wind, while the Muslim sailors, a mile behind, sat becalmed in searing heat.

"It was said that sweet dreams, along with the fragrance, preceded the robbers and announced the saint's arrival at Venice. The doge welcomed the sailors as heroes. There was a huge celebration. Money was collected. The grave robbers became wealthy men."

"Where did the good smell come from?" Mark asked.

"According to the legend it was a miracle, proof of the saint's sweetness," the doctor said. "Venetians adopted Mark's emblem as their own—the winged lion standing with a front paw upraised, jaws open. It wasn't long before the Lion of Saint Mark, embroidered in gold on a brick red field, fluttered from every masthead, and by the doge's order the lion's head was carved on every wellhead.

"Get ready," said the doctor. "We're coming up on the square."

10

Blindman's Bluff

The Piazza San Marco was like a glittering box, its red, peach, and yellow painted walls studded with ornaments and flags. There were tubs of trees and blooming plants around cafés with tables outside, each place with its own little orchestra squeaking away, trying to play over the milling din of hawkers selling crosses and bottles of holy water. There were Japanese tourists in plain dark coats, Buddhist monks in capes of carmine and saffron, priests from Greece in large black hats, Russians in furs, tour groups clustered around flag-bearing guides hollering through loudspeakers in strange languages.

The great doors of the cathedral stood open. The inside glowed with gold and candlelight. Chanting and singing drifted out in waves, music of Christmas.

"You could go in alone," the doctor said. "They won't let me in with Boss."

Mark was hesitant. He didn't like crowds. "I'm fine just looking at the outside."

"Okay," said Doc. "We'll skirt the crowd and get a good look from the doge's palace, over there," Hornaday said, pointing.

They walked to the far side of the piazza, to the pink and white building at the edge of the lagoon where the Grand Canal began.

"Here's where they set the spring that shot Marco east," the doctor said. "Here's where the doge in his gold-embroidered robes and what looked like a stuffed animal on his head schemed over maps."

Hornaday leaned against the wall. "When we were kids," he said, "we made make-believe telephones out of two tin cans and a piece of string. We'd punch a small hole in the bottom of each can and run the string through, knotting the ends. With the string pulled tight, the listener would hold his can to his ear while the speaker shouted into his. You could make out something, but it was muffled.

"I picture the doge yelling into his can here while Kublai, thousands of miles away, listens to his. Marco is the string stretched tight between them.

"Squint," the doctor suggested. "Pretend you're

Marco, sitting on that stone dock over there watching a long war galley from Constantinople approach, sails down, her sides rough and dark with bits of seaweed caught in clots of pitch and tar and loose caulking. Her deck shines like metal, freshly washed and sanded.

"Picture her entering the Grand Canal, passing the immense coil of gleaming chain they kept ready in those days to be stretched across should enemy ships approach.

"The oars flash together like centipede legs as the ship's boy beats time on his drum and the captain bellows *'Ohi! Ohi! Ohi!'* to warn off smaller boats. Chained to the mast, a black African and a pale Russian study the eyes studying them.

"See those two columns at the edge of the square? Those are the seamarks sailors landing at Venice looked for. On top of one a saint stands with his foot on a crocodile. Saint Mark's winged lion is on top of the other.

"In Marco's time strolling musicians played for money here as wealthy merchants and their wives and men and women of court paraded slowly in embroidered silks and rich velvets, flashing their jewels and lifting their robes slightly to show their fine pointed shoes. Some wore thick gold rings set with diamonds over brightly colored kidskin gloves.

"Suddenly the crowd stills. A prisoner is brought to the dock in a black gondola.

"Punishments and public executions took place between those landmark columns—flogging and branding for stealing, heads chopped off for murder. It's said to be bad luck to walk there.

"This prisoner's crime was not so great. He got locked in a wooden cage and hoisted partway up the gray column. People teased and threw cabbages and fruit at him until workers came and set up the gaming tables again. Within minutes the merchants and nobles were rolling dice and slapping down cards as they roared out their stories, everyone talking at once like an opera and nobody minding."

The doctor looked at his watch. "I've got to run an errand. How about I drop you at your hotel for a lie-down? On the way we can look at the merchants' palace they'd never have let Marco into—the place with books about silk growing on trees and dog-headed Chinese."

Boss gave the doctor a look.

They caught the pitching waterbus to the Rialto Bridge. The lagoon water smelled like the ocean; it was gray, not green like the canal water.

Boss looked forlorn, head down, his paws spread wide to keep from falling as the boat plunged and yawed.

Mark moved close and hugged him. "I'll steady you," he whispered.

Boss licked his face. Mark smiled. No dog had ever had a chance to do that before, and he still wasn't sneezing.

Every quarter mile or so the vaporetto would stop like a land bus, honking the smaller boats out of the way. A sailboat was luffing in the channel, unable to move. The bus swerved wide as the sailboat pitched crazily in the wake.

The merchants' palace was white and grand like a Greek temple, with columns out front, carved gargoyles, and medallions. There was writing over the entrance.

"What's it say?" Mark wanted to know.

" 'Let all who trade here do so honestly,' " the doctor translated.

"Did they?"

"Ha!" said Hornaday with a sharp laugh. "*Caveat emptor*—'Let the buyer beware'—has always been the merchants' rule, but the doge and his council had regulations to keep things fair and protect the reputation of Venetian goods. They checked quality, weights, and measures. It wasn't unusual to see smoke rising in the market square when the governors discovered defective cloth or some bad spices and ordered the stuff burned.

Public examples like that kept folks honest, because the doge's men didn't just burn what was bad; they torched the cheater's entire stock."

"Okay if Boss stays with me?" Mark asked when they got to his hotel.

"Sure," said Doc. "I'll meet you at one for lunch at the signora's."

Mark and Boss headed upstairs to Mark's room. As Mark slid the Chinese pillow under his head, the dog floated up and lay down beside him, uttering a long whistling sigh of joy as he stretched out full length. But a few minutes later, Boss began to jerk and twitch in his sleep, quivering, his teeth chattering. A bad dream! Mark put out his hand to comfort him.

Boss awakened, looked up at Mark, then licked the boy's hand in gratitude, sighed, and went back to sleep. Mark lay there watching in case the nightmare came back. It felt good being needed. He'd never felt that way before.

He was tired but he wasn't sleepy. His mind was going all over the place, sights and images boiling around in his head like the flakes in one of those snow globes.

Gradually the swirl of ideas settled on one thing: St. Mark's. Seeing the light shining out, hearing the music—he had to get inside to see what Marco had seen. He had to go back. He had some money, and his mother had given him a book of vaporetto tickets.

Boss was suddenly wide awake, ready for whatever Mark had in mind.

The boy tried to leave word with the hotel clerk, but when the man saw the dog again, he scuttled back into his night closet.

They caught the waterbus and rode down the Grand Canal to the San Marco stop.

The crowds in the cathedral yard were thicker than before. Mark gritted his teeth. There was a wall of people he figured he'd never get through.

Then he noticed a display of Italian sunglasses on a souvenir cart. It gave him an idea.

He went to the cart and tried on a pair. He checked them out with Boss. The dog nodded.

Mark gestured to the man and said, "I'll take these."

"Twenty euro," the man said.

Mark pulled out what he had in his pockets: thirteen euros plus the book of vaporetto tickets.

"You have anything cheaper?" he asked.

"No," said the man. Then he smiled. "What you have there—the money and the tickets—I sell them to you for that, Mister Hollywood."

Somehow from behind the glasses the crowd wasn't so intimidating.

Mark took hold of Boss's collar. The dog led him toward the open tourist gates slowly and deliberately, his great plume waving, his blue tongue out and slobbering as he grinned and hooted his way through the crowd.

They got to the great doors.

Mark nodded to the dog. Boss sat down, prepared to wait for Mark for as long as necessary. Mark let go of the leash and merged with the warm, shuffling tide that sounded like silk rubbing on silk.

He was in. He pulled off the glasses and waited while his eyes adjusted to the smoky dim. There was organ music and singing far away. The space was huge, the domed ceilings soaring higher than anything he'd ever seen. The slanting winter light coming in from one side was golden, touching the mosaic pictures in the domes over his head. There was Noah tenderly helping a pair of long-necked green and turquoise birds into the ark while others just as gorgeous but azure with white dots waited their turn. And then, farther on, there were the merchants in their little black boat bringing back a long casket with the bones of Saint Mark over a vivid sea of black swirls on gold. As the boy stared, he could almost feel their boat pitching and heaving over the deep.

He had goose bumps. The hair on the back of his neck went up. "Marco," he whispered. "You were here. You saw those sailors, you knew the story, you could feel the water. Maybe you stood right where I am now." He shivered, but he wasn't cold.

Moving deeper into the dusk and hush of the cathedral, it felt as if he were walking in the hold of a great ship, moving up toward her prow. He became aware of the incense and candle smoke. It was heavy to breathe. There were trays of candles in niches along the sides of the cathedral, their light flickering off paintings, polished panels of marble veined like old wood, columns carved like spirals and capped with bunches of leaves, relic boxes on stands—some made of crystal edged with gold, others of ivory and carved stone—each filled with a holy object or martyr remains. In one, he saw what looked like a circle of rusted barbed wire on a faded silk pillow stained with what might have been drops of blood. In the next, he saw a Bible bound in jewels with a broken blade smashed into it. In another, there was a skull with auburn hair and teeth and beside it a severed hand.

He walked slowly toward the high altar, where Saint Mark's bones were kept.

Everything was polished stone, even the uneven

floor that dipped in some places and rose in others so sometimes Mark caught himself stumbling. The stones were laid in patterns so confusing he had to look up. As he did, he saw a figure like the signora's Madonna smiling in a niche, only there wasn't any paint splashed on her. She seemed to be smiling at him, nodding.

"My dad," he whispered. "Please, Lady, watch out for him."

He moved with the hush of shuffling worshipers up the stairs to the high altar. It was covered with embroidered silks, a tall golden crucifix in the center, on either side smaller jeweled religious ornaments and a pair of tall candelabra. There were mosaic figures on the sides, glittering in vivid colors outlined in black and gold. The music was close now, men's voices chanting from above. The light was hazy, as if pouring through fine golden dust. The incense was dizzying.

He made his way to a pew and sat down. Overhead there were images of angels. No one was sitting close by, but it felt as if he wasn't alone.

Maybe Marco sat here, he thought, *with his aunt and the cook and everyone for Christmas Mass.*

Suddenly he was cold. He remembered Boss. He stumbled out. Boss had made himself small in a corner by the door beside a tiny old gypsy woman who was crouched there begging. Mark gestured that his pockets were empty; he had nothing for her. She understood.

The dog led him away.

Mark was broke. They had to walk back to the signora's restaurant.

Dad,

Doc is some doctor. I'm a lot better. He can tell stories almost as good as yours. I've been to St. Mark's. There was a big crowd, but I got in. I saw what Marco saw. It's really something! Doc's dog helped me get to the door. His dog is named Boss, and he really is boss. He's really big and he doesn't make me sneeze. I haven't seen Mom all day. She's at the agency. I hope she's getting them to find you and give you my letters. If they do find you, will you let them bring you out? I hope so. I miss you a lot.

Love, Mark

11

A Secret Mission

Mark and Boss were waiting at Signora Eh's when Doc came in. As they finished eating, Doc rolled up his napkin. "Who sent Marco to Kublai?" he asked.

Mark was surprised. "Didn't he go with his father and uncle as a merchant to trade? Or for the pope? He says in his book they carried a letter from the pope, so maybe the pope sent them?"

"They traded as they went along," the doctor replied, "but I don't think that was their main purpose. Marco reports what goods were available, but he never talks abut trying to make converts or gloats about making a good bargain. Other merchants' journals are full of brags about the deals they made, but we don't get that from him, and we don't hear much about the pope's letter either.

"No, I think they were on a secret mission for the

doge. He wanted permission for Venetian merchants to use the Chinese spice ports. He figured that would give them a real edge over the Genoese."

Mark shook his head. "If he really was on a secret mission for the doge, why didn't he say so?"

"Because he'd been sworn to silence," the doctor replied. "Years later he figured it was okay to tell what he'd seen, but to say why he'd gone, who'd sent him, and who paid for everything—that would have given away too much to the Genoese, so he never did.

"The way I see it, the doge needed someone to go in secret to negotiate with Kublai. Marco's father and uncle turned up at just the right moment. They'd met Kublai, after all, and the doge trusted them. They'd been giving him secret information about the East for years."

"You mean they were spies?" Mark asked.

"Not exactly," the doctor said, "but merchants make good informants. They remember what they hear as they nod and listen over cups of liquor and piles of money. Gossip and bargaining have always gone together. Without your knowing it, a good merchant can talk you into anything.

"The way I imagine it," he went on, "late one night a man came to Ca Polo with a sealed message. It wasn't signed, but from what the messenger hinted, Marco's father guessed it was from the doge. It directed him to go with the messenger to meet someone who would arrange his voyage to China.

"They went by boat to the marshy island where the Jews had to live, Giudaico—'Jew place.' The doge's messenger led them to a darkened house.

"The man knocked. There was rustling inside, then the door opened a little. There were whispers. The Polos slipped in like shadows. The man who'd brought them stood guard.

"The Jew they were sent to meet was there with his brother. They lit candles and unrolled a map of the route Chinese junks sailed.

"Marco's father had never seen such a map. It was better than anything in the doge's palace. It was exact and detailed. It had been painted on paper at Kublai's court.

"Kublai ruled his empire from maps like that. He'd long since given up trying to ride his boundaries; instead, he ran his finger across his maps, giving orders, directing lives and roads and crops a thousand, two thousand miles away.

"The Jew gave the map to Marco's father along with a note introducing him to the Jew's friends and relatives and asking that they arrange the Polos' passage to China and give them slips that would serve for gold as they traveled.

"The visitors never sat down. The whole business took five minutes in hushed voices."

"Why all the sneaking around?" Mark asked.

"Because the doge didn't want anyone to know what he was trying to get from Kublai, and it wouldn't look good if word got around that he was relying on the Jews for help. Jews were looked down on in Venice in those days, but they could do things in the Middle East that other Venetians couldn't. They had connections with Arab merchants and caravanners, and they had contacts in the Indian and Chinese ports. Their links of friends and family could arrange payment from Egypt to China without moving a ducat. Gold was heavy and dangerous to travel with; the Jews paid each other with slips of paper. They lived by the old expression 'Travel light and you can sing in the robber's face.'

"The Polos got ready to go. They'd sail to China with a letter for Kublai from the doge. They'd see if they could talk the emperor of the East into letting Venetians use his port.

"If he wouldn't, there'd be trouble when they got home. The doge didn't look kindly on emissaries who failed."

12

How Marco's Story Got Told

The café was almost empty by the time Mark and Doc finished their pranzo. The signora brought Boss a plate of scrapings—cheese rinds and sausage ends—and sat down, sliding her feet out of her slippers. She began rubbing one foot with the other.

"So," she said. "Your Marco Polo, where is he now?"

"Setting out for China," answered Mark.

"Ah!" said the signora.

Boss stretched out with a long sigh. Mark slipped off his shoes and put his feet on the dog's warm back. A wave of good feeling swept over him.

"Here's how I picture it," the doctor began. "The doge had the Polos carry gifts to Kublai—pieces of Venetian glass and a big silver mirror framed with jewels so the emperor could admire himself. The Polos' own luggage was what they figured they'd need for a voyage of three or four years—which is as long as they planned to be away.

"When everything was packed, the boatmen came to Ca Polo with handcarts, yelling and calling back and forth like opera singers. Feathers flew up as they dropped the bags and boxes into the hold of the waiting workboat that earlier that day had carried chickens to the Rialto Market.

"The Polos rode with their things to the convoy dock on the Grand Canal. The galley they were going in swallowed their goods like nothing.

"The merchants' families stood together, saying little. Then a rattle of drums, and trumpets sounded and the galleys swung out, sails rising, oars swinging to the now slow thumps of the drummers in their blue wool uniforms with bright gold buttons.

"Marco stood on deck and never looked back," the doctor continued. "He looked east as if he expected to see Kublai waving to him in the distance.

"They landed at Acre, the great Crusaders' fortress on the Mediterranean near Jerusalem, where the Polos collected the pope's letter of greeting to Kublai and his gifts for the emperor—carved crystal goblets and a portable altar of silver with cups and plates of gold for serving Mass.

"Before dawn his first morning at Acre," Hornaday

said as he rose slowly, "Marco heard the *muezzin* calling the followers of Islam to prayer from his tall spike tower beside the blue-tiled mosque.

"Heijahijah!" the doctor cried as loud as he could, his voice warbling up and down.

Boss leaped up, barking as the remaining diners turned and stared. Hornaday smiled and waved and sat down again. "Five times a day," he continued, "the Muslim faithful are called like that to wash their hands, faces, and feet before prostrating themselves facing Mecca—the place sacred to Islam—to chant their prayers.

"The walls of the mosque were tiled with designs in grays, black, and white. The tiles in the side rooms had bright-colored medallions and patterns of plants, seeds, flowers, and arabesques. The prayer rugs all over the floors had similar decorations in shades of purple, pale slate, blue, rose, and green, with touches of dark yellow and cream. Because Muhammad had forbidden making man's image, no tile or rug had human figures or faces.

"Marco's father translated the beautiful Arabic writing they saw in glowing blues and eggplant purple on the tiles and inscriptions on public buildings everywhere: 'There is no God but God, and Muhammad is His prophet—' "

"Wait, Doc," Mark interrupted. "What's the difference between Islam and Muslim? Where does Muhammad fit in?"

"Followers of Islam are called Muslims and Muhammad is the founder of Islam," the doctor explained.

"So," he resumed, "the Polos signed on with a caravan bound for Hormuz. Their plan was that once they got to Hormuz, they'd sail to China in one of the huge Chinese ships called junks. They were the largest ships in the world at that time, piloted by Arab navigators using pieces of magnetic iron floated on bits of straw in bowls of water—the first compasses.

"But they got to Hormuz too late. The fleet had left. The monsoon winds had shifted and begun to blow away from China. The Jews had gone without them. The letters and maps the Polos were carrying were useless. They were stuck. Should they wait a year for the next sailing or head off on the Silk Road?" the doctor asked.

"That's what they wanted to avoid," Mark said. "The road was really dangerous, especially the southern route through the Gobi, where Dad is."

Hornaday nodded. "But Hormuz was an awful place, hot and sickly, so they decided to take their chances on the road. They signed on with a caravan and hired riding camels. The grizzled Arab who pocketed their gold gave them a long look up and down. 'Men of white meat are little apt for warm weather,' he muttered grimly.

"They stained their faces with root dyes and walnut juice and oiled their hair and bound it back in bright cloth so they'd look like the men they'd be riding with. They wore Arab cloaks—but was anyone fooled by their costume? The desert Arab notices everything—the slightest variation in cloths, a mend in a foreign thread—he can spot a stranger just like that," the doctor said with a snap of his fingers.

"The sheikh who led them," he continued, "was a tall man in a loose tan jacket and a length of embroidered silk twisted around his head. He wore a broad green skirt with an elaborate woven belt. At his waist at the front he carried a *scimitar,* the curved dagger of the nomads as long as a man's arm. His was inlaid with silver."

Hornaday reached into his coat and pulled out a gleaming scimitar with snakelike curves worked into the shining metal.

"I found it in the Christmas market coming over here this morning," he said, handing it to Mark. "Another piece of Marco's world for you to go with your pillow. Merry Christmas!"

"Wow," said the boy, studying the knife and testing the edge. "It's really sharp! Thanks, Doc."

"Let me have it back for now," Hornaday said, standing up and tucking the knife into his belt. "It's part of my costume."

The dog looked up as the doctor wound his red scarf around his head.

"You give us a show?" the signora asked.

"Doc's the caravan guide," Mark explained. "He's going to take Marco across the desert."

"Good," said the signora. "Go!"

"To the clatter of leather drums strung with bells, the Polos set out," the doctor said. "Marco was better mounted than most, on a dark orange camel with a rough, lurching gait. No camel is smooth-gaited like a horse. With her head high she shuffled along. To make her turn he was taught to tap her head gently in the direction he wanted to go; to get her to stop and let him down, he would rap her neck until she sank to her knees."

I've seen that camel! Mark thought. *On the front of that building!*

"That first day Marco was really sore," the doctor was saying. "A camel's back is broad—broader than a horse's—so he had to spread his legs wide. They rode until late.

"When at last the halt was called, Marco dug a

shallow hole in the sand, rolled up in his cloak against the sudden cold, and lay down. Three hours' sleep, then the boom of the sheikh's gong and off again.

"As he got up, Marco rolled on a scorpion that had come close in the night for warmth. The bite left him sick for days, his shoulder swollen—"

"Hold it, Doc," Mark interrupted. "Are you making this up?"

"I'm imagining how it might have been," Hornaday explained. "I'm imagining from how it was for me when I was on the desert going to Kirkuk."

He went on. "The Polos were traveling with a merchants' caravan. Nowadays, we have goods from all over, things so cheap and plentiful it's hard to imagine how eagerly villagers in Marco's time listened for those travelers, and the cheers that went up when they heard the traders' camel bells clanking miles away.

"Wherever they stopped they'd hand out treats of dates and dried cherries to the children and let the women admire themselves in Kublai's mirror. For the men there were pinches of clove and cinnamon, for every girl a tiny drop of oil of rose from Persia to dab behind her ears. For the little ones they'd knot twists of brightly dyed wool into tiny figures."

"To make friends as they went along," Mark said,

getting the idea. "They were outnumbered. They needed friends to watch out for them in case they got in trouble. Dad brought trinkets with him to give away too." *In case he gets in trouble,* he added silently.

"The villagers didn't have money," the doctor continued. "The few things they bought, they traded for—eggs, cheese, and chickens in exchange for needles from England and a few bright glass beads.

"They didn't make a fire when they stopped at noon. Lunch was a greasy cold ball of cooked millet left over from breakfast, a raw onion, maybe some slices of dried apple, all of it washed down with fermented milk, stuff like our yogurt only smellier. The smell came from the goat stomach they carried it in. When a pack animal died, they'd butcher it on the spot and feast on roast meat until it got putrid—at least the men with good teeth would. It was tough and stringy. To keep awake they gnawed balls of sheep fat mixed with pounded green coffee beans. The poorer men—there were no women in the caravan—carried small greasy bags of cloth or leather stuffed with fruit scraps, lumps of millet and bread, cheese rinds, chunks of hardened yogurt, bits of meat and fat left on the bone, any sort of butter. In the heat and pressure of travel, the mess would congeal in the bag. At the break they'd claw out chunks and work them in their mouths, spitting out what was too hard or foul to swallow.

"Those traders were dream merchants," the doctor continued. "They didn't expect to make money from the villagers. They stopped and gave them gifts because they liked giving pleasure to wide-eyed children and dark-haired women.

"At night Marco sat with them, cross-legged, around the cook fire as they twanged long-necked stringed instruments, played wooden flutes, and sang the epic of the desert in high voices—songs that sounded like groans and moans, their voices going up and down as if they were crying or dying. Sometimes a few of the men would dance together, very slow, no matter how fast the music.

"As they approached any town of size, the traders would ring their biggest bells and put on gaudy capes of red and purple so the people would know they weren't the ordinary peddlers of pickles and hides; they had things from far away and dolls with yellow hair and painted faces. Those dolls always sold better than anything."

"Is all this in Marco's book?" Mark asked.

"No," said the doctor, shaking his head and smiling. "Some of it is my imagining. Everyone who reads *The*

Travels adds to it and makes it his own—which is how *The Travels* came to be.

"See, Marco Polo didn't write his book," the doctor explained. "After he got back to Venice, he was asked to be honorary admiral of a galley in a war with Genoa. His was one of ninety Venetian ships that sailed out for the sea fight—flutes, trumpets, and kettledrums going, the crews singing as hard as they could to keep heart and strike fear into the enemy. It was a disaster. The Genoese sank or captured most of them.

"Marco was lucky to be captured. Hundreds of his fellows drowned. He was hauled off in chains and locked in a dungeon.

"He waited in prison, scared and lonely, hoping that someone at home would buy his freedom."

"Did he sleep in chains and fight off rats?" Mark asked.

"Maybe not that bad," Hornaday said. "Marco's jailors wanted to keep him alive to get their ransom price, but all around him men were dying of untended wounds and jail fever. It was dark and filthy. The food was swill with bits of rotting meat. Every day the jailors dumped thirty or forty bodies into the sea.

"This man who'd been so famous in China—Kublai's favorite—'Marco Milione' of Venice—was just another prisoner in the dungeon.

"Some people lose their minds when they're thrown in upon themselves like that," the doctor said. "A few—Saint Paul, Cervantes, Nelson Mandela—save themselves by telling or writing their stories. It's a way to confirm who you are, what you were, to create something out of the awful nothingness of prison life.

"Marco told his story to a cellmate.

"The man he told it to was a well-known writer of stories named Rustichello. He wrote *The Travels* from what Marco told him. The style is Rustichello's—the style of the King Arthur legends that were popular then—but the urgent tone of the book must owe a lot to Marco's desperately spinning the threads of his past to escape his present."

"How did he get out?" Mark asked.

"Somebody finally paid his ransom," Hornaday said. "But it took a year. Maybe the Genoese heard his nickname and held out for a big sum.

"The way I imagine it," Hornaday continued, "Marco sent home for the notes he'd made for his reports to Kublai. He and Rustichello then used them to work up *The Travels.*"

"Does Marco say he took notes?" Mark asked.

"No," said Hornaday, "but I think he must have as he traveled—notes for his reports to Kublai. The book is too detailed for him to have told it all from memory.

"As Rustichello wrote down Marco's story, he added things he thought would please his readers. That's why we don't know if it's all true. Like I said, everyone who's ever heard Marco's story has added to it, making it his own.

"It was before printing, so when Rustichello got out of prison, he sold handwritten copies of the book he called *Description of the World.* We know it today as *The Travels.*"

"Did Marco get a lot of money for it?" Mark wanted to know.

"Nothing beyond the pleasure of having his story go around," the doctor said.

"Why didn't he write the book himself?" Mark asked. "Why did he just give his story away?"

"Because he was a teller," Hornaday explained, "not a writer. People who tell stories rarely write them. We don't have a single sentence Marco wrote himself."

Mark grinned. "Or any of his notes, right?"

"Nobody's ever seen them," Hornaday said with a laugh, "but maybe someday somebody like you prowling in an ancient room in Genoa will come upon a falling-apart bag of Venetian leather, and in it . . ."

Mark pictured himself in a dusty, gloomy room like the basement of his hotel, opening what looked like an old suitcase, and there were Marco's notes, small shapes of intricately marked paper fluttering out like butterfly wings.

"Over the years," Hornaday was saying, "people made their own copies of what Rustichello wrote. A lot got changed. More than a hundred different handwritten versions survive, so we don't know what's closest to the story Marco told."

Mark nodded. "So did people start to believe Marco after his book came out?" he asked.

"No," said the doctor. "He was always something of a joke in Venice. Now he has rooms in the museum, but then? No. I think Messer Milione died a joke."

The signora pursed her lips and shook her head.

"Marco Milione, tell us another lie," she said. "A person always carries his mask in the Christmas pantomime, and always someone calls to him, 'Another lie, Marco! Give us another lie!' "

13

To the Court of Kublai Khan

"What did you hear about Dad?" Mark called out as his mother walked in.

"The herders are all changing their grazing routes to find water," she said. "That's why they can't find him—because they can't find the shepherds either. But they're optimistic."

Mark guessed this was good news, but his mouth was dry and he had to force himself to eat. He wanted Doc to get on with Marco's story so he could stop thinking about his dad.

By the time they finished dinner the café was nearly empty. The signora was rigging a string of tiny white lights around the window with a loop circling the Madonna.

She brought over a plate of biscotti, a pitcher of orange juice, and a glass of red wine for the doctor.

"Be comfortable," she said as she sat down with them.

"The doctor's going to tell us how Marco goes to Kublai," Mark said.

"Ah," said the signora, nodding. "In school for the little ones at this season the children do the *mimica,* acting the story of Marco Polo without words. They put on costumes and masks and pretend to be the travelers and the beasts. The biggest boy, he is always Kublai; the next biggest, Marco. The girls are always the camels, but in my class," she said with a giggle, "there was not so many boys and they was small, so we say no, the boys are camels now. I was the biggest, so I was Kublai, king of the East."

She turned to Hornaday. "Doctor, please, the story."

Hornaday wrapped the red scarf around his head again and, with a growl, whipped out the scimitar and flashed it close to Mark's face. The boy reared back with a sharp cry.

"Now I am an Arab caravan leader," Hornaday began as he tucked the scimitar into his belt.

"When we left our travelers, they were fleeing Hormuz. Open desert was better than that oven of smoke and dust. They set out across the desert of Syria. The land became drier and emptier.

"Even with a four-hundred-pound pack, a camel

can go twenty-five, fifty, maybe even sixty miles a day for four or five days without water if there's grazing. They get moisture from the greens they eat. Their mouths are tough inside, and their teeth sharp, so they can even eat thornbush and get water from it, but where there's no grazing and no water, they go down after three days.

"Late on the third day Marco's caravan came to an oasis where the water was so foul-smelling no man would touch it. Camels, though, can drink stuff that would sicken you and me, but at this place it was so bad the drivers had to cover the beasts' noses and force open their jaws to make them take it.

"If she's willing, your camel can suck up several quarts a minute. To water a camel that won't suck it up herself takes a lot of work—hauling five or ten heavy goatskins of water from a sandy oasis hole, then forcing it down the gullet of a big bubbling, roaring beast that will bite you if it gets the chance.

"It was four days' hard march to the next oasis. The heat, sand, and pebbles were wearing down the pads on the camels' feet. The pad is what makes the camel such a perfect sand traveler. It works like a snowshoe, keeping the camel from sinking into the sand, but it can wear thin and suffer cuts from sharp stones. A limping camel is a dying camel. On the third day, two of the caravan animals failed. It was a close thing whether the rest would make it.

"The caravan chief made his men go dry. He doled out the last water to the grumbling beasts. At dusk on the fourth day, they saw the outlines of palms against the dark. He brought them stumbling into a water place at the edge of a green plain.

"At this village they exchanged their worn-out camels for donkeys, mules, and horses and headed into the lowlands of Persia.

"They came to a *caravanserai,* an inn set behind high mud walls built around a well with a watchtower in one corner. It was a government station for merchants. There was a locked warehouse where they could store their goods.

"These inns had been built a day's walk apart, with stalls and fodder for the animals, rooms for the travelers, food—all free to make the merchants feel safe and encourage commerce along that strand of the Road of Silk.

"The innkeeper kept incense burning because the merchants and the men tending the animals did not wash. There was little water and no soap. People wore filthy clothes and coated their hair, faces, and the exposed parts of their bodies with rancid grease and mineral pastes to guard against the sun and cold and the constant biting flies that could eat a man's eyes out in hours. The travelers stank.

"Marco's room was a low square of mud brick with a narrow slit window. Against one wall there was a raised platform of dried mud—the *kang,* or bed. The floor was a hardened paste of ox blood and mud. Hungry ticks, fleas, and lice awaited him.

"The keeper showed Marco an ancient writing someone had left behind—a bundle of thin strips of bamboo tied together and inscribed with Chinese characters from top to bottom. The characters were blurred and worn from many readings by passing travelers. It was a piece of scripture, what the Buddhists call a *sutra.*

"'You, lad,' the keeper said, 'you know the art. Read!'

"Marco couldn't. He didn't know Chinese. But rather than disappoint, he repeated what Mustafa had told him about the sound that monks make when they read the sutras.

"'It's a sacred Buddhist text,' he said, 'a sutra too worn to make out, but if I could—if I read it the way the monk who wrote it did—the holy chant would sound like purring.'

"He made a loud purring sound—*ommmurra-aaaah*—like that," he said as Boss lurched. "*The cat is reading the sutras* is the Chinese phrase for purring.

"They proceeded east," the doctor continued, "higher and higher through grasslands where they sheltered with herders who lived in yurts—dark, greasy-looking, six-sided tents made of felt and skins rubbed with fat to keep out the rain. It was cold. They huddled with a herder's family around the dung fire in the center of the yurt. There was no chimney. Only some of the smoke made it out through the hole in the roof.

"At this place they bought fresh horses, short,

sturdy mounts like the ones the Mongol raiders had ridden as they'd accompanied their interpreter some years before—horses that lived on the roots and grass they scratched up as their hungry riders cut open a leg vein and drank their mounts' blood."

Mark made a face.

"Now they began the long climb," the doctor was saying. "In the mountains of Afghanistan they hired yak pullers as guides and yaks to carry their baggage—powerful, patient animals with shining black coats so long and shaggy they drag on the ground.

"Alive and dead the yak is valuable: his coarse hair is woven into stout cloth for outer garments; the thick hide makes sturdy boots and thongs for tying tents. The females give rich milk; the meat is ground into sausage; the horns are carved to make utensils and knife handles. The tail they keep as a prize," the doctor said, reaching into his coat. "The yak tail is the symbol of the Mongol leader."

Mark heaved back as Hornaday swished the hairy wand around. "A souvenir of one that served us," he said as Boss sniffed and frowned.

"You ate the rest of him?" Mark asked.

"We did," said the doctor, "and I bet Marco's party did the same.

"The men rubbed their faces, hands, and necks

with yak butter," he went on, "slathering it on as thick as they could to keep off the sun and keep out the cold.

"Their trail zigzagged up and up along the mountainside. At some places they had to clear the way of ice. The air grew thin; the cold wind cut like blades. The horses would take a few steps, then pause while their knees shook and their heads drooped. The yaks panted, their breath whistling.

"The drivers slit the beasts' nostrils so they could get more air. They treated the cuts with a white paste they carried to stanch the bleeding.

"At dusk they'd dig pits in the snow big enough for two or three men and cover it with a dome of snow blocks, leaving a side hole just large enough to crawl through. They'd light a yak-fat candle inside. The candle's heat and that of their bodies would melt the snow overhead, so pretty soon the inside of their hut was sealed with ice and almost warm. If someone's feet got really cold, he'd put them against his partner's bare belly as the other rubbed his legs to get the circulation going.

"One afternoon a blizzard of numbing cold stalled the horses. Some of them froze stiff in place with their riders. One could tell the rider was dead if his teeth showed, the lips drawn back in a grin.

"At noon the next day a yell went up from the lead men. They'd come to a gap—a five-foot section of road had slid away. There was rock wall on one side, a steep drop on the other. There was no going around.

"The wind was blowing snow.

"'We leap it!' the guide hollered.

"With shouts and coaxing they got the horses over, but when it came her turn, the lead yak balked. She was carrying a heavy pack. She went to the edge and looked down. She wouldn't jump.

"The guide backed her up, tightened his hold on the cord through her nose, thwacked her hard on the rump, and began to run as everyone yelled and pushed. He leaped across; she followed, eyes closed, her front legs tucked up as if she were diving. Had she balked again, or gone down, the guide would have plunged to his death."

The signora gasped. Mark's heart was pounding.

The doctor went on. "The wind tore at them, making their fingertips split, their lips and cheeks crack and bleed. That night they sheltered under rocks. The ice crust was too thick for them to dig pits in the snow.

"The next day they pressed on, gasping in the thin air, sometimes hanging on to the tails of their horses, forcing the beasts to drag them up the icy steeps, scooping out pits in the snow to rest.

"Marco grew weak. He'd been feverish for days. Then one afternoon he fainted and fell off his pony.

"At that place in the mountains he nearly died. The air was thin, he couldn't get his breath, he had a chest infection—probably pneumonia—and he was sick in his gut with parasites and worms. He'd been weakened by a year of constant travel, bad water, and poor diet.

"A shaman came, a priest who uses magic in his cure. He came with a great black dog."

With a woof, Boss heaved up and nearly overturned the table.

Doc nodded and went on. "The shaman was old. He wore a flat black hat and a yak-skin coat. He brought a wand with tiny bronze bells and jingles, and a small drum painted orange and red with figures of animals and men in black. On his shoulder there was a bag of embroidered silk stuffed with garlic, rhubarb root, dried herbs, mushrooms, moss, lichens, and scrapings of mold—a primitive form of penicillin.

"He waved the wand and started beating his drum—*tap tap tap,* like this," said the doctor, hammering out a slow rhythm on the table with his spoon and fork.

"He circled around his patient," Hornaday said, "faster and faster until Marco grew dizzy watching as the old man drummed and skipped and danced and sang himself into the spirit world. His mouth was foaming when he fell to the ground clutching the wand as his drum rolled off toward the fire.

"After a while he got up. As the spirits instructed, he prepared a stinking red gruel. The rhubarb root in it worked as a purge for worms. He had to pinch Marco's nose to get him to swallow it. Then he made him eat clove after clove of garlic."

"Argggh!" Mark went. His stomach churned. He felt he was there with Marco, shivering and nauseated.

"And you complain about the stuff I give you," the doctor said to Mark.

He continued. "Once the shaman had forced his medicine down Marco's throat, he lit sticks of harsh incense and began a howling chant.

"His medicine had weakened the bad things inside Marco. Now his singing made the spirits come and draw the sickness out.

"Marco was purged—his guts were empty—and the shaman's medicine was working in his chest, but the treatments had left him weak and shivering.

"He was frightened and depressed, ashamed about holding the others back. He was about to give up. It went through his mind that it would be better—easier—to die, just slip away in his sleep.

"That's when the shaman's dog saved him."

Boss rattled his tags.

The signora smiled and pointed down. "Like that one, yes?"

Mark nodded, smoothing the great head at his feet.

"Without being told to do so," the doctor said, "the shaman's dog lay down beside the sick boy to give him warmth and courage.

"When the old priest left, his dog stayed. From that day forward the dog lived with Marco, following him everywhere."

Mark reached down and scratched Boss's ears.

"Marco lay half-dead for weeks. It was a long time before he could travel again.

"As they rode slowly down out of the mountains nearly a year later, they came to a place where they were met by Kublai's royal escort. The emperor had gotten word of their approach. Nothing happened in his kingdom that he didn't hear about as fast as men could sprint and ride.

"Early in his reign Kublai had ordered the roads improved and marked with cairns and signposts and a smooth center lane laid out for himself. Trees had been planted for shade and windbreak and post stations built every twenty-five or thirty miles, each with horses and riders ready at any hour to hurry news to the emperor or to bring him some rare fruit just ripened in some distant province.

"Between the post stations there were foot runners waiting at three-mile intervals, each wearing a belt with loud bells so the runner at one stop could hear another approaching and snatch up the message bag midstride like a relay racer.

"In this way Kublai learned overnight about wars and floods ten days' march away as he ate the first ripe peaches.

"During the last forty days of their trip, the Polos rode on post horses and fed well with the soldiers at their post stations as they made their way to the emperor of the East at his summer palace at Xanadu.

"It was early in the morning and cold when Marco stood with his dog, his father, and his uncle at the entrance to Kublai's tent.

"They had washed and dressed carefully. The young Venetian wore polished maroon leather boots, black woolen hose, and a bright blue cloak of finest English wool. It came to his knees. His skin was pale compared to the Mongols', his eyes round and hazel-colored, while theirs were black and almond-shaped. His hair was brown and curling; theirs was straight and black.

"The huge dog knew to hang back, but the Polos all started to go in together. The guards stopped the older ones.

"Marco was ordered to go in alone.

"For a moment he stood in the doorway, unable to move.

"At that instant Mustafa came to him in a vision and hissed in his ear, 'Pretend to be brave even if you aren't. It's eat or be eaten with that man, so keep him off balance. Do not try to amuse him; confuse him. In no way seek his friendship or protection. Pretend to be immune to any threat, safe from any danger. Go!'

"Marco went in."

14

Marco Meets Kublai

Boss began his long kowtow wake-up stretch as the doctor stood up slowly, like a big stick figure unkinking. "It's late. Time to shove off," he said, pulling at his turban. "Come on, boy."

"Hey!" Mark protested. "You can't stop there!"

"No! No!" the signora exclaimed. "No matter how late, we must hear."

Hornaday shrugged, emptied his glass, and sat down again. He was like a performer called back for an encore.

"If you say so," he said, taking a deep breath.

"Kublai's summer capital was in Mongolia. It was a walled park sixteen miles around in the high grasslands. At the center there was a palace, but Kublai preferred living in something that reminded him of the tents of his childhood. The palace of marble with columns and ornaments was for his people: they loved dazzle; it made them feel strong. He didn't need that; he preferred the white tent of felt and bamboo he'd ordered set up in a field of tall steppe grass.

"At the entrance to Kublai's tent, two of his biggest guards stood with iron rods beside what the Mongolians called a humbling bar, a knee-high stick visitors had to step over.

"The height of the bar signified the occupants' rank and compelled respect, since crossing it required one to bow, and the higher the bar, the deeper the bow. It was also believed to keep out ghosts because ghosts couldn't bend their knees.

"Mongol men were shorter than Europeans. They wore heavy fur coats that brushed the floor. They were careful about crossing the entrance bar, but sometimes a foot or a coat hem touched it. Nothing was supposed to. Touching it was considered a bad omen. If a visitor tripped or misstepped and touched the bar, Kublai's guards would strip the offender and whip him, and he'd have to pay to get his clothes back.

"Marco was tall; he floated over it. He was twenty-one.

"Kublai's tent was supported by six white poles, gilded and banded blue and topped with carvings of dragons like the ones on Mark's pillow. The ropes were white silk. There were blue panels in the roof with the constellations figured in silver at their positions on the longest day of the year. The room was fragrant with roses.

"The emperor of the Tartars sat in a white silk robe on a carved wooden bench cushioned with a scarlet rug. He was shorter than Marco, muscular, the color of tarnished copper. His skin was sleek, like it had been oiled. His square face shone behind a long black mustache and a skimpy clutch of brushed chin whiskers. His ears were long and pink, the lobes white and fleshy. It was said that his great ears caught every secret. His chest was broad; his arms were thick. His hair was tucked under a white skullcap tied tight with a thick black band. His eyebrows were tapering gray lines high above his eyes, which were half-closed. When he opened them wide, they cast light. It was said that the secret of his power was in his burning eyes. His mouth was small, his lips thin, the teeth small and yellowish. He was fifty-eight.

"He wore no jewel or ornament of office. He didn't need to; you saw him and you knew you were in the presence of power.

"In front of his throne a thick cord of silk hung from a tent pole. When emissaries came from neighboring tribes to pay tribute, Kublai would invite them to climb it. Few could. He would laugh and pull himself up hand over hand without effort. He called for challengers at rope climbing. No one had ever come forward.

"A broadsword crusted with dried blood, flesh, and hair lay against his bench. A strong man would have needed both arms to wield it; Kublai managed it with one. When news came of any challenge to his authority, he would take his sword, slash off the end of his climbing rope, and send the stump to his enemy as he set out after him. Most fled or died; Kublai took no prisoners.

"Marco stepped forward and bowed in the European manner.

"Kublai was surprised. He didn't know what to make of this young, close-shaved European who bowed but did not kowtow.

" 'Are you a priest?' the emperor asked in Persian. 'I sent for priests and teachers.' He spoke slowly in a high-pitched voice.

"Marco knew enough Persian to understand and answer. 'No, Sire,' he said in a level voice as deep as he could make it.

" 'Are you a teacher?'

" 'No, Excellency.'

" 'Are you a merchant?'

蒂姆

" 'No,' said Marco, struggling to keep his voice steady.

" 'What are you, then?' the Mongol yelled, half rising from his throne.

"Marco was respectful. He was scared, but he tried not to show it.

" 'Eyes, ears, nose, fingers, and memory,' the slim Venetian replied, touching his eyes, ears, nose, and forehead as he spoke.

"Kublai caught his breath and stared openmouthed. Was this rudeness?

" 'Of those I have thousands on thousands,' he snarled. 'I ask your pope for a hundred teachers and all he sends is a sharp-tongued stripling?'

"The emperor pursed his lips so they bulged out purplish. He stared hard at the young man standing calm before him. The hotter Kublai got, the cooler Marco felt.

" 'All right, Eyes, Ears, Nose, Fingers, and Memory, speak!' Kublai growled at last. 'Tell what you have met coming here!'

" 'I will, Excellency, and I will be grateful if you, in turn, will tell me why, with your thousands on thousands, you have asked for a hundred of our teachers?'

"Kublai reached for his broadsword to cut down

this impertinence. Then he caught himself and laughed. His laughter was like barking. 'Speak, Venetian!'

"Marco began to describe his trip.

" 'We started our journey by water, Excellency, five weeks' sailing from Venice to Acre. We traveled in convoy, ten of our long black ships. In an evil fog conjured by pirates, we were attacked off the coast of Palestine. We lost a galley and ten of her crew, but we gave better than we got. We holed two of theirs.

" 'After we saved our own, I was for picking up their drowning, but our captain said no. "I'd sooner take scorpions aboard," he said. "Those men are drugged and heedless of life. They'd do everything they could to take us over, even at the cost of their own lives." So we left them gagging on their fate.'

"Marco's voice was slow and soft like the low notes on a flute, not shrill and fast like the high-pitched Mongol voices Kublai was used to.

" 'At Acre I went into the buried temple where they store water, so even in the dry season they have plenty. We went to the fountains where those faithful to Muhammad bathe their hands, face, and feet five times daily before prayers and after being with a Christian.

" 'I ate the sweet dried fruits of that place—raisins,

currants, sultanas, dates, and figs. I touched the tall carved stone Alexander placed to point his way east. The men there squat to pass their urine in the manner, we were told, of the prophet Muhammad, because they wear skirts.'

"Marco paused. Kublai waved his hand. 'More!' he mumbled.

" 'We set out over the desert of Syria on camels, past a place where there are lions and excellent mines of salt and the people wear on the head a cord ten palms in length that they wind around it.

" 'Before noon that first day, my skin was blistered and my eyes ached from the glare and glittering. Our guide gave me charcoal mixed with sheep fat to daub under my eyes to ease the glare.' "

Mark drew a ragged breath and tried not to think of his father fighting the desert light.

" 'We met the wandering people called nomads, who follow flocks and live in round tents of woven hair. As their flocks move, the women collapse these tents and load them on two-wheeled carts. They can do this in an hour. It is said of those people, "The fatherland is the tent and the backs of their horses."

" 'We traded for the weavings their women and children make,' Marco said, reaching into his coat, 'weavings of wool dyed green, purple, and other colors they press from the roots and flowers of that place.' He pulled out a small tightly patterned rug. 'A present, Sire.'

"Kublai grunted as he took it.

" 'Go on!' he muttered as he studied and pulled at the small rug. The colors were soft, the knots small and tight. It was fine work. As he smoothed it on his lap, Marco noticed his hands, clean and perfectly shaped, the nails long and polished.

" 'We passed into Iraq, Sire, and came to a place where there is a spring of oil not good to eat but good for burning and as a salve for men and camels afflicted with itch. This oil, too, I brought you,' Marco said, digging in his pocket for a small jar.

"Kublai reached for the gift.

" 'Be careful when you open it, Excellency. The smell offends.'

" 'I know,' Kublai replied as he uncorked the jar and sniffed. He jerked his head back. His eyes began to tear.

"Marco pretended not to notice as Kublai rubbed his eyes and cleared his nose, blowing hard, thumb to nostril, then wiping his nose on his sleeve.

" 'We came to the ruins of a great city conquered by your grandfather,' Marco continued. 'We were told the people had surrendered without resistance, but then he herded them outside the gates and massacred every one—even their dogs and cats—and ordered every dwelling knocked down. We wondered at this, since they did not resist. . . .'

"Kublai's face showed nothing.

" 'There were brightly colored parrots there, my lord. I brought you the feathers of the brightest one—these orange and green ones.'

"Kublai took the clutch of feathers and spread them out on top of the small rug, toying with them and arranging them as Marco spoke.

" 'After many days we came to the gulf of Persia,' Marco said. 'At the great harbor of Hormuz, where all the goods of the East are sold, we'd planned to sail with your China fleet in one of the great masted ships.

" 'We arrived too late. We missed their going on the wind that blows your ships home from that place. It would be a year before the next eastward going.

" 'We were offered a boat they make there, but their vessels are small and badly made, the planks lashed together with coarse thread. Those boats leak. We heard that sometimes in the fierce storms of the Arabian Sea, the cords break and they sink. We Venetians know ships, Excellency; these we would not board.

" 'The sun at Hormuz is so hot, Sire, tar melts and

runs from what it's meant to seal. The city is made even more unhealthy by the killing dust that blows in from the desert. These winds affect foreigners most severely because they don't know how to hide from them. Despite all precautions, many die of the *simoom,* as it is called, and in hours their bodies rot to shells. Also, we were warned that if a foreign merchant dies there—as many do—the king takes all his possessions for himself.

" 'The water we were offered was teeming with worms, so in our thirst we drank the wine of that place. It is made with dates and spices. It made us sick, or perhaps it was the salt *tunnies*—tuna—they sold us to eat.

" 'For us Hormuz, with its evil winds and food, was an unwholesome place, and the king's way with strangers ominous, so we left, paying a huge price to join a Silk Road caravan and bribing the sheikh every few days not to abandon us.

" 'At one point it was a near thing. We were camped outside a village. The *imam*—the local holy man—came and squatted with our sheikh, eating his broiled dates and drinking deeply of the fiercely spiced date wine. Suddenly this priest threw down his drinking pot and exclaimed, "This is what comes of consorting with infidels"—traveling with non-Muslims, Christians, is what he meant. "You disrespect your brothers. I curse you," and with that he rode off.'

"The emperor narrowed his eyes and nodded.

" 'We passed in the direction of the sunrising and the Greek Wind into Persia and went north and east to meet the Road of Silk where it rises into the mountains. It was early autumn when we left the plain; in the mountains it was winter; rain and sleet at first, then snow and winds sharp with ice. On the steeps we had to dismount, sometimes clinging to the tails of our horses and whipping them so they'd drag us up.

" 'Our toes froze. The horses wheezed. Many died of falls and exhaustion. For days we traveled where there was no shelter, sleeping in pits we scooped out of the snow and covered as we could. No birds fly there and fire is not as bright nor of the same heat as elsewhere. Our rice and lentils would not soften; the meat we boiled stayed too tough to chew. I could not get breath.

" 'I grew weak and feverish, my skin dried to parchment, blood came from my nose and bottom, my lips cracked and swelled, my pulse raced. It felt as if my heart were trying to jump out of my chest. At the summit of the highest pass, we stopped to place a stone on a cairn. Travelers do this for luck. I fainted and fell from my horse. They tied me on. I shook like one in a fit.

" 'Our road passed an empty temple to the Buddha. They laid me in it and built a fire by the doorway. There was no chimney. I was smoked. I was in a daze.

" 'One morning I awakened to bells tinkling and the warbling of a conch horn. An ancient monk had come to honor the Holy One in His temple. This priest wore a dark orange robe, patched and filthy. I thought I was dead and he was from the spirit world until he gave me a sweet smile that I should live.

" 'He sent a doctor of his faith to heal me.'

"Marco stopped talking.

"Kublai stared at him, his face like a turtle's, unblinking.

" 'What medicines did the shaman give you?' the emperor asked.

" 'He healed me with magic and chants, jingling bells, drumming, dancing, incense, and mold mixed in red gruel.

" 'I brought you some of his potion,' Marco said as he handed up a stoppered bottle of clear glass banded with black swirls.

"Kublai turned the bottle in his hand.

" 'The glass is a product of my city,' Marco explained with pride. 'We make all manner of glass there.'

"Kublai had seen such things before but none so delicate and finely banded. 'The effect of this medicine?' he asked.

" 'I don't remember, Sire. They say I slept for days. I know I woke in a sweat as my fever broke, but for a long time—weeks, months—all I knew was that it was a place of tall fir trees. I could see their tops swaying in the wind from where I lay. The fragrance of those trees was the purest scent I ever smelled.

" 'My illness held us back for a year.'

" 'Ah,' said the emperor. 'And you are strong again?'

" 'Yes, Sire.'

" 'So the medicine was good,' Kublai announced. 'You will go back there with my guards and seek out that priest. You will bring him here with his potions.'

"He signaled that one of his secretaries should make a note.

" 'Go on with your getting here,' Kublai said as he turned the small bottle of medicine around and around on top of the parrot feathers.

" 'Coming out of the mountains, our caravan descended across the long dry plains,' Marco said, 'then into the grasslands, where we met people who raise horses and live in tents made of their hair. My father traded with them for fresh mounts, and they gave us savory steaks of horse meat and the drink they call *koumiss* made from horses' milk. Our most valuable trade good to them was salt.

"'For some days we went on, swooping lower and lower like a bird descending as we approached the desert.

"'We were met by a party of dervishes, the wandering monks of Islam who take a sacred vow never to cut their hair or wash it. They wear bright rags and carry spears, Sire, sometimes walking, sometimes dancing.

"'They are said to be priests, but our guide warned that many are thieves.

"'We gave them alms. They gave us news of the locals. As we passed on, they gave the locals gossip of us.

"'They warned us there were land pirates on the sea of sand we were meant to cross to reach you. They sold us an amulet for a great price to make those pirates afraid.'

"'What amulet?' the emperor demanded.

"Marco held out the small clay figure of a draped woman.

" 'And did you see these land pirates?' Kublai asked.

" 'No,' said Marco.

" 'So this kept them away,' Kublai said, juggling the tiny clay woman in his hand as if it might burn him.

" 'Go on with your travel,' he ordered.

" 'The traveler enters the Gobi at the oasis town called Lop, Sire. The first sign of its water is the vulture hanging in the air, waiting to drop on the dying camel or traveler approaching from the other direction who cannot make the last mile in.

" 'We refreshed ourselves there and gathered supplies for our month-long crossing of the desert. The winds blow strongly at that place and lift clouds of dust and silt into the air, giving it a yellow haze. They eat rat there, Sire, and consider it a great delicacy, gutted and roasted in its skin with garlic. They eat lizard and boiled dog as well.

" 'But you rule this land, Excellency, so I will not burden you telling about it.'

" 'Tell!' snapped the Tartar. 'If you can surprise me with news of what I know already, perhaps I will let you live.'

" 'Tomorrow, Sire,' said Marco, turning to leave.

"It was forbidden to turn your back on the emperor. It was an even greater offense to leave Kublai's presence without his permission.

"The guards approached, their iron rods raised to strike.

" 'Stay or die!' the emperor hissed.

"Marco turned back. 'Does the caged bird sing as true as the wild?' he asked quietly. 'Never mind. Kill me, and my stories end. I am tired. I will return tomorrow.'

"The Venetian's heart pounded. He imagined the guards' blows and the wind of Kublai's great sword as it fell to sever his neck. But he held steady. This was how Mustafa had told him to end his first audience with the great leader of the Mongols.

"Again he turned away.

"Kublai's guards moved closer.

" 'No,' said Kublai, laughing in his high barking way. 'Let him go. He knows no better. Or perhaps he knows very well.'

"Marco's visit left Kublai restless. There'd been a time when he'd been quick and brash like Marco. Now he felt heavy and burdened. He called for his horse and his ten strongest companions. Together they galloped hard into the park his hunters kept stocked with wild animals. Kublai was a fierce rider and reckless hunter. He lived for danger; only when he risked his life did he feel alive.

"They cornered a tiger. Kublai jumped from his

horse and took it on with his black lance, the blade inlaid with gold.

"The beast crouched ten feet away, hot with fury. Kublai had one chance. If his blade missed the heart, he'd get mauled before his men could save him.

"With a scream he hurled the lance.

"The blade went true. Red showed on gold."

15

On the Gobi

Hornaday paused, pulled the scimitar from his belt, tested the blade, tucked it back, then adjusted the red turban.

"Leaving Kublai's tent," Hornaday resumed, "Marco was escorted to the lodge for imperial guests. Visitors to Xanadu—diplomats, noblemen, high-ranking tribute-bearers, Persian merchants, Arab traders—were all put up in this compound. His father and uncle were bunked together with the others, but Marco was given a private suite furnished with every luxury, layers of fine rugs, sheets woven with silk and wool to sleep on, a marble tub for bathing, and every delicacy Mongols knew. His great dog lived with him, sleeping beside him, eating what he ate.

"Marco was comfortable enough—this was better than kangs and snow pits—but he was never alone.

Fluttering, light-footed women in bright silks brought his food and bathed and dressed him. A hidden minder watched him always.

"At noon the next day Marco was summoned back to the white tent. He prepared himself carefully. He rehearsed his speech about the doge's request.

" 'Continue the story of your getting here,' Kublai ordered as Marco stepped over the humbling bar.

" 'The doge's letter, Sire,' Marco began. 'His gifts . . . Your reply—'

"Kublai's roar cut him off. 'My reply? My reply? I do not reply to *you,* Venetian! Tell as I demand!'

"Marco forced himself to stand tall and take a deep breath as he pushed his hands tight against his sides.

" 'We set out across the Gobi,' he began, 'all shale, boulders, and wind-driven sand that shrieks as it washes away tracks and landmarks.' "

Mark pictured his father somewhere out there. It was as if the doctor were telling his nightmare of his father lost in sand waste, the wind making eerie screams, the awful emptiness, his thirst. The boy's breath came short. His hands were freezing. He looked at his mom; she'd gone pale.

Boss snuggled close to his legs.

The doctor kept on. " 'We'd bought what our guide said we'd need to get through that place of fire and cold.

" 'At its narrowest, the desert takes a month to cross. No one has ever gone its length. It's all worn-down mountains, sand plains, sudden sinks. There's nothing to eat. If your guide is lucky, you will find water, but sometimes the underground course shifts away from where you expected to find it, or what you come upon is so bitter with salts you cannot swallow it. Other times you arrive at a well that was promised to be good only to find it fouled with camel waste from the last caravan.

" 'We were told by a seller in the market we should wear red to frighten off the dragons. Another said, "No, the dark absorbs the sun. White is better." So we bought from both. By day we wore white; at night, when dragons roam, we wore red. We daubed our mounts' necks with goat blood as demon repellent.

" 'That first merchant was splendid-looking, with a curly black beard, slender nose, and large black eyes. On his head was a wide turban, green, with a half-moon of coral pinned on. Perhaps his wife was just as striking, but all we could see of her were ragbound feet at the bottom of a dark red bag with eyeholes. I don't know how she got air enough to breathe.

" 'Our guide was dark. He was not young: his braided hair was streaked with gray. Such of his face as we could see was all lines and hollows, and what teeth he had were brown. His forehead was low and broad, his nose high and hooked. He wore a long-tailed, tangerine-colored coat with wide lapels that he could fold up to cover his face. The coattails he tucked into heavy pink trousers, which in turn were tucked into tall, pale blue boots. He slept in a tent of white cotton trimmed with red and green.

" 'His constant companion was a large white rooster, by day chained to the saddle, pitching uneasily, balancing with his large white wings. At night he roosted unchained on a post at the front of his man's tent. His feet were huge, with long curving yellow claws.

" 'One night a thief tried to sneak in. He ran off screaming under battering wings and rooster claws that cost him an eye.

" 'That rooster was the only pet. The scavenger dogs that followed our caravan out of Lop were soon eaten.' "

Boss shifted uneasily.

" 'The guide's deputies wore red tunics under black cloaks. They carried the long curved knives of the desert and slept outside on rugs. At night they took turns chanting the epic of the desert together, the same three notes deep and slow in their throats.

" 'It was like this, Excellency,' Marco said, looking down at a square of paper in his palm.

"He began to chant in his deepest voice like those men had, a long piece of music that sounded like crying.

"When he stopped, he looked up.

"'Perhaps you know this music, Sire?'

"Kublai was wide-eyed. No man had ever sung to him before.

"'Perhaps,' he muttered. 'Perhaps, Venetian. Continue.'

"'Our caravan was forty camels, Sire. Camels stink. Their spit is foul. If you annoy one, he will spit his juice at you and attempt to bite. The bite of a camel is an evil thing, deep and hard to heal, quick to infect.'

"Kublai nodded and pulled up his sleeve to show a jagged purple scar on the fleshy part of his upper arm. 'A camel bite,' he said.

"Marco glanced at the wound and shrugged as if it were nothing—as Mustafa had advised him to do under such circumstances.

"'The evening before our departure,' Marco continued, 'the serving men, all slaves, stuffed pillows and blankets of felt under the camels' saddle frames so they would not rub. Those frames would not be lifted until the beasts returned four months later—if they returned at all.

" 'Upon the harnesses of the lead camels—the tall ones they call pilgrim-camels—there were shields of scarlet with metal mirrors at their centers. Their ranks of bells sounded with each footfall—the sound of the march.

" 'We were warned to watch for spiders and snakes and to oil our bodies against the sun and the biting flies—especially around the eyes, which is where the flies strike in swarms, for the eye is always moist.

" 'We were told to keep away from places where the sand looked wet, no matter how thirsty we were, for it is not water: it is quicksand, the loose sucking sand that swallows men. No camel will go near, but mules will, and thirst-crazed men. Many thirsty are lost at those places.

" 'We were called before dawn by the booming of the chief man's great bronze gong, a disk the size of a cart wheel worked with strange figures in silver and hung with silk thongs on a long pole. It is so heavy, two men are assigned to carry it, while a third—a squat knot of muscle with a hardwood club—stands on a box and strikes with all his strength. It is said those three are deaf from this work.

" 'It goes OOOOOOOOMM,' Marco bellowed as hard as he could, bringing Kublai's guards stumbling over each other."

Hornaday's yell had Boss up and barking as the listeners clutched each other.

" 'There was a great hubbub of making ready, calling and running with lanterns, striking the tents, then a confused roaring of men and protesting of camels.

" 'Another great OOOOOOOOMM and we were under way!

" 'We marched out of Lop two abreast, swaying and jerking on the slow-footed camels through green that grew sparser and sparser until there was none, just sand and empty wastes of gravel. Sometimes a heap of

stones marked the way, sometimes graves, sometimes what our guide called "heaps of witness"—a place where someone had a vision. The desert is a great place for visions.

" 'The track swung down into a depression they call the Valley of the Demons. Dried camel dung and skeletons marked our track. The slaves collected the dung for our cooking fires. There was no other fuel. Dung burns hot.

" 'We were told to curb our thirst. We were drinking in a morning what a desert Arab drinks in a day.

" 'Half of our fleet of "ships of the desert," as those humped beasts are called, Sire, carried our water in goatskins—bloated hairy carcasses, the legs tied off at the feet, the crotch stitched tight, the neck corded off.

" 'There was a long stretch where, as we'd been warned, there was no water, so we drank from those skins. The water was cloudy; it slimed on the tongue and had the taste of fish.

" 'It was six days' march to the next oasis.

" 'The dawning sun glowed and made the desert fragrant. Two hours later its light smacked us like the flat of a sword. There was no color. We saw no living thing except the flies that pricked at us, trying to drink our eyes.

" 'Sometimes gusts of wind come that groan like dying men. We looked at each other: were there people out there we should rescue?

" 'They are the lost dead, according to our guide. You hear the ghosts of ones who could not keep the track, or their camels grew weak and could not get up.

" 'We were warned, too, about the evil demons in the desert. They shriek and wail. We were told it has happened that travelers going to see if there is someone in distress have been lost, for those sounds are not men but the voices of spirits and goblins. Sometimes the spirits will call a man by name.

" 'Sometimes there are sudden storms of sand driven by a burning wind, Excellency. The old camels sense it coming and begin roaring and going to their knees, stretching their necks out long and laying their muzzles on the sand.' "

Mark was gripping his seat.

" 'We were caught in such a storm, Excellency. There was thunder and lightning. Quickly we formed the caravan in a circle around the lying-down beasts and wrapped the animals' heads and our own in cloths so we would not breathe in the sand—particles as fine as the perfumed dust your slave powders you with after your bath, Excellency.

" 'The animals groan deep in their throats as you huddle tight together, gasping in rags, chewing grit, the stuff filling your shoes and sifting in where your pants meet your shirt and your shirt your neck. It flies up your cuffs into your armpits and your nether parts, where it rubs and chafes.

" 'We lay down flat lest the spears of lightning strike us as they have struck many beasts and men there, peeling off their skins.

" 'The hurricane moves swiftly and passes in a moment, but if the beasts and their men did not protect themselves, they would die an awful choking death.

" 'The dust can suffocate a man in an hour, the sun

can cook him in an afternoon, thirst will finish him in a day—his tongue swollen and black at the end. Hunger kills in a week—but the snakes! Their bite finishes a man in minutes.

" 'We met them wherever there was water—puff adders, cobras, black snakes. At night we walked with sticks, beating the bushes to drive them off. When all was quiet and no one was moving about, these serpents would slither up silent to lie close against us for warmth. With care we rose to obey the calls of nature. The first to rise would search around his fellows with a stick. One morning we killed twenty.

" 'The chief's men hurried about collecting all the snakes killed in the night—often a great pile! For breakfast they'd gut them and chop the lengths into sections and roast three or four in a row on the tips of their long curved knives. The meat was white. It tasted like rotten chicken. They counted it a great delicacy. I threw up the piece I ate.' "

Mark paled. On top of what the doctor had just said about the dust storm, the thought of eating roast snake made him want to gag. He swallowed hard.

Hornaday kept on. " 'When we stopped at night, our first task was to dress ourselves and our camels with the black oil of Arabia against the itch. Once the camels stopped walking, the itch was all they could think of, so we did what we could to keep them from going mad with it. Where their packs chafed we eased them with butter. Only when a camel went down dying did we remove its pack, and then the men would fall upon the beast with their knives, hacking it apart for food.

" 'Mine was a red she-camel. At one point, exhausted and thirsty, she stumbled and fell down a sand cliff, throwing me hard. She lay whimpering and trembling. For all my yelling and prodding she would not get up. I was sure she'd die there.' "

Mark nudged his mother. "A red one, like what we saw on that building," he whispered. She nodded.

" 'Roaring a terrible curse, our guide circled back and swung off his camel. He slid down to where mine lay moaning. He dug in the baggage and pulled out the pelt of her recently dead calf.

" 'He held it before her. She sniffed and rose. He led her up the cliff. I mounted and we went on. She never failed me again.

" 'That night we made some miles in the dark, but we were tired and hungry. We stopped to camp.

" 'The next day the wind came on again. We made but few miles. Our goatskins were going flat.

" 'The guide said, "We soon pass water holes marked by cairns. Drink what you find there and you will void your bowels ten times over."

" 'He ordered, "Now you will save your urine. It will not hurt you to drink it. The camels will not. We give them what is left in the skins. To you the taste will be the same."

" 'We did this, Sire. The taste of a man's urine is the taste of death.' "

Mark shuddered. "I am going to be sick," he groaned.

Hornaday went on. " 'We were not eating now, Excellency. We slept on our bellies to ease the hunger ache and keep them from swelling. Two days farther on, still without water, we saw what looked like a wet place in the sand. Despite our warnings, one man ran limping toward it, his hands cupped. The quicksand caught him. He stumbled and began to sink, flailing and howling. Before our rope could reach him, he had sunk to silence.

" 'The desert is searing hot by day with such intense bright light, the only way to survive is to wrap yourself in white suits and head swaddles. Evening comes on with fiery hanging clouds. Then, quickly, it is freezing cold under gleaming stars so bright the Arabs make maps of them.

" 'In Venice we do not see such stars. In the desert

there are no clouds. With so many stars it is easy to find bears, rams, shepherds, and see the Magi approaching overhead.'

"'Magi?' Kublai asked. 'Who are these Magi?'

"'The wise men who came from Persia to see the infant Christ. They were summoned by a brilliant star. It is in the Bible.'

"'Such things happen to many in the desert,' Kublai muttered. 'The sun cooks their brains. In the dark they have visions. Go on.'

"'At the other side of the Great Desert there are mountains, and the green begins again. Dug into those mountains there are hundreds of caves honoring the Buddha, each one with a painted image of him or a carving of his figure, some with images of the lesser figures as well, all gilded and painted in vivid oranges, crimsons, grays, and blues before scenes of gardens with beautiful women and animals.

"'Flames gutter before these figures day and night on twists of wool in bowls of fat. A thousand crimson-robed monks tend them, chanting, ringing tiny silver bells, clanking hand cymbals of brass.

"'These monks beg their livings from those entering and leaving the desert. Those about to depart give them alms in hope of good fortune; those arriving give by way of thanks for their safe coming.

" 'The rest you know, Excellency. The monks gave us cups of their thin soup, and for a small coin they allowed us to sleep in a temple, but all night long they sing-songed and sounded their bells. Their singing was like the desert winds of the lost.

" 'The next morning, Sire, forty days from here, your soldiers met us.'

"Marco stopped speaking.

" 'More!' the emperor commanded.

" 'I have no more to tell, my lord.'

" 'More!' the great man boomed. 'More!' "

16

A Great Miracle

"Marco held his face steady.

" 'There is nothing more to tell, Excellency,' he said in a level voice. 'Everything here is strange to me.'

" 'What is the strangest?'

"Marco thought for a moment.

" 'The paper, Sire,' he said at last. 'In Venice paper is a rare thing. We write our books on skins. Here your daily edicts are painted on sheets of it. Even in the place of relief there is paper for wiping.

" 'But strangest of all is your black money paper. I don't mean the magic money—the tokens painted to look like coins that the Buddhists burn with their dead so the spirit will have funds in the next world. I mean your real money.

" 'Our doge collects tribute and taxes in gold and silver as you do, but unlike you, he must pay out the same to his servants, soldiers, shipbuilders, and provisioners.

" 'I am told you pay all those you owe with these different-sized slips of black paper stamped with your vermillion seal, and no one in all your kingdom is allowed to make or spend any other money.

" 'The wonder is your people accept those scraps. I see in the markets that even the rumpled ones buy grain and oil and all the other necessaries of life.

" 'Your shadow gold works like real, but in fact it is worthless, my lord. Since it has no value, why do people take it?'

"Kublai smiled. 'It has value because the people believe it does.'

" 'Today, yes,' said Marco, 'but what if tomorrow they stop believing in that trash?'

" 'Venetian,' Kublai muttered, 'your tongue is a dangerous little muscle. One day I shall have it out. For now, though, tell me the one thing of Venice you miss the most.'

" 'I am tired, my lord. . . .'

" 'The one thing, then you may go.'

" 'The music of the street, Excellency.'

" 'What music is that?' Kublai asked.

" 'People laughing and speaking words I can understand as the women stand in their doorways and talk to one another and the men idle slowly together to the taverns at dusk and stand arm in arm, telling each other stories.

"'I miss the bells of Venice, Excellency. Your huge bells clang the hours and alarms, but there is no joy in their sounds. Our bells have silver in them, so they ring with a sweet mellowness. Our smallest ones tinkle like young girls laughing. From dawn to dark we hear the music of our bells calling us to prayer, to work, and to rest. I miss our bells and hearing the monks sing our prayers. I feel deaf here, as if my head were wrapped in wool.'

"Marco caught himself. Hadn't Mustafa warned him never to show his feelings?

"*'Sounds?'* Kublai asked, pulling at his thin beard. 'Of all the things of Venice, you miss her sounds the most?'

"Marco nodded.

"Kublai shook his head and turned away. Marco got up to leave.

"Kublai swung back. 'No! You may not go yet. You must first tell me about a wonderful thing of Venice—something I do not know.'

"'You said I might leave once I'd told you what I missed the most.'

"'I expected to hear about something I'd want!'

the emperor screeched. 'Your noise of Venice is nothing. Tell me about something I might want; then you may leave.'

"Marco took a deep breath so as not to show surprise. His mind was blank. His heart was pounding. Then it came to him.

"'Very well!' he exclaimed with such force the emperor's head jerked back and his guards jumped. 'Send those men for paper, brush, ink, and a small table.'

"Kublai clapped and barked the orders.

"When all was in place, Marco rubbed his hands together and sat down. 'I will show you one of our great miracles,' he announced. 'Those huge sheets of paper you order hung on your palace walls every day—your official decrees—each as long as a man is tall, filled with hundreds of the beautiful picture characters that make up your language to say a simple thing. To fashion them your clerks must work many hours painting. I am told there are thousands of those characters.'

"Kublai nodded.

"'Here are ours,' Marco said as he proceeded to write out the alphabet. 'These few Roman characters: A, B, C, D . . .' Taking up another sheet, he said,

'Look, Excellency, see how our miracle works. The heading on each of your proclamations is two arm lengths across. Watch as I write it in our characters: *Kublai Khan, Emperor of All East, Decrees . . .*'

"He handed the sheets to Kublai. 'Everything that could ever be said or thought, Emperor, you may express in one arrangement or another of these letters.'

"Kublai squinted as he studied the marks.

" 'Enough perhaps for simple people,' he muttered, 'but for us who think more deeply, more is required.'

" 'No,' said Marco with a thin smile.

"Kublai lurched back. No one was allowed to say no to him, but Marco pressed on.

" 'Everything you can think to say we can express with these—even the thoughts of the great philosopher Confucius—we can express his subtlest thought in these few letters.'

"Kublai glowered. 'You lie, Venetian! Prove what you say! I take nothing at mouth value.'

" 'For now you will have to take my word,' Marco replied. 'But someday you will send a scholar to Venice and he will learn our language. He will come back to you with all of Confucius in our few letters.'

"Kublai made an ugly face and spat.

"Marco turned and left.

"The emperor flexed his immense arms and climbed the rope to ease his restlessness. He missed his ranging warrior life. He missed the freedom Marco had to travel.

"Not that Marco was really free," the doctor said. "He could travel throughout the emperor's territory, but he couldn't go home. His company was too valuable for that."

"He was a prisoner?" Mark asked in a tight voice as Hornaday stood, unwinding the turban.

The doctor raised his eyebrows and nodded.

"Then how did he get away?"

"He almost didn't," the doctor said.

Dear Dad,

Is the Gobi as bad as Doc says? Do you have your own camel? What color is it? Doc says some of them have curls like girls' hair on their necks. Do you watch out for her feet? He says that's really important.

Is there anybody like Kublai in charge where you are? I miss you a lot. I thought it was going to be a really bad Christmas here alone with Mom, but I've made friends with Doc's big dog, and Doc gave me a curved knife like the caravan guys carried on the desert. Is there Christmas where you are? Will you give the herders the knives and stuff you took? I hope you are OK.

Merry Christmas!

Love, Mark

17

His Impertinence Beards the Emperor

Waves of Christmas fragrance met Mark and his mother as they started down the sixty-eight steps the next morning. Swags of balsam fir and spruce hung from the spikes and rings in the dark walls at the bottom. In one corner there was a basket of silver wands and twisted sticks covered with tiny red lights. The lights made the room glow.

As they pushed open the heavy door into the street, they met people laughing and calling to each other as they bustled along carrying flowers, parcels of fresh bread, and brightly wrapped presents.

Doc Hornaday and Boss were waiting for them at Signora Eh's.

"After breakfast," Mark said, "I want to show Doc something."

* * *

Later a chill wind gnawed as Mark led Doc and his mom along the canal.

"There." He pointed.

At that moment the sun came out just as it had the first time he'd seen it. The camel on the front of the building was handsomer and redder than he'd remembered. Doc had never noticed her. Mark was proud to be the one to show her to him.

They studied her from the calle, then they walked up to the next bridge and crossed over the canal for a closer view.

"She might have been Marco's camel," Doc said. "She's two-humped, a Bactrian—the kind they used on the Silk Road. Her humps were filled with fat—served as her gas tank. She carried water in her stomach. Camels don't need much water because they don't sweat or pant; they just let their bodies get hot. Temperatures that would kill us are nothing to them. It can get to over one hundred thirty degrees out there."

Hornaday studied the carving. "The artist who carved her really knew his camels," he said. "Look at those eyes! I bet if we could get high up and close, we'd see her long curling eyelashes that kept out sand. Camel eyes inspired a lot of poetry."

"Why's she up there?" Mark asked.

"Maybe the merchant who built that palazzio owed his fortune to her," the doctor said. "Maybe she carried him across the Gobi with jewels sewn in his coat, day after day in searing heat with no water as the other beasts failed. . . ."

Mark imagined his father somewhere out on the desert in searing heat with no water. Was a camel saving him?

They headed back. The lanes were full of people now; all the shops were open. They walked slowly, looking in the shop windows.

Suddenly Mark's mom grabbed his arm.

"Look!" she exclaimed. "The sign on that mask: 'Marco Polo—Il Milione.' There he is, Marco the Millionaire."

It was the bright pink face of a darkly bearded man. His hair was pulled back in a ponytail. He was smiling a big smile, his small teeth spaced far apart. He wore an earring shaped like a Chinese character. The mask came with a gold-colored sack stuffed with fake jewels.

She hurried in and bought it. "To go with your pillow and the doctor's knife," she said as she handed it to Mark. "Put it on tonight when you lie down on that pillow. Maybe you'll have Marco Polo dreams."

I already do, Mark thought.

He put the mask to his face.

"Yes!" his mother and Doc exclaimed together as they stared at him.

Boss yipped and wagged.

Back at the café Mark turned to the doctor. "Where you left off last night it was Marco's second day at Kublai's court. What happened?"

Hornaday settled right into it. "That morning Marco got up at dawn. A line was forming outside the palace, ordinary people, men and women, rich and poor, in every sort of costume. Who were these people?

"When Kublai got to the palace, he read the dispatches his night riders had brought; then he listened to his generals' reports and the clerks' accounts of wheat yields and taxes collected. Next the tribute bearers were allowed in with presents and rarities. Finally came the reports of what his people needed."

"Like what?" Mark asked.

"Funds to repair a washed-out bridge, grain where a harvest had failed, relief from taxes. And teachers: they were always asking for more teachers.

"What interested him most, though, were the appeals of individuals—the people waiting in line outside. Every hour court servants went down the line offering slices of dried apple strung on a cord and a skin of koumiss with a drinking horn. The alcohol in the koumiss helped keep them warm and alert.

"If one of those waiting had to leave the line to obey a call of nature, he would signal to an attendant, who would stand in his place until he returned.

"Kublai quickly dismissed the generals, clerks, and tribute bearers. Then he called in the people waiting outside. For them he had endless time.

"They came asking him to judge their complaints, some from far away. Their disputes were about family matters, land shares, inheritances. Most quarrels like that were settled by the local chiefs, but if a party did not feel justice had been done, he could appeal to

Kublai. Some did it in song, the rhythm of verses helping them remember the points of their case."

"But how did they get there, Doc?" Mark interrupted. "You said some came from far away."

"They came by horse on the post roads like the one the Polos followed to Xanadu," the doctor explained, "resting in the stations where the soldiers quartered. There was a law that each local governor had to arrange free passage to the emperor for anyone wishing to present a grievance.

"Kublai didn't hurry these petitioners. If a person's speech was foreign or stumbling, he called for interpreters. He listened with care. He had a good memory. When he ruled, he always explained his decision.

"It was well past noon when the last petitioner left the palace and Kublai returned to his tent. He summoned Marco.

" 'Tell me more about crossing the Great Desert,' he ordered. He had never been there, and he was eager for more of the strange Venetian's talk.

" 'I have finished that, Excellency,' Marco replied. 'I have told you—'

" 'No! More!' Kublai exclaimed, half rising from his bench. 'Something you did not tell me before.'

"Marco shrugged and settled himself on the floor

at Kublai's feet. This was another of Mustafa's calculated affronts. No one ever made himself comfortable in the emperor's presence, but before Kublai could protest, Marco had begun to speak in a voice so soft Kublai had to lean forward to hear—another of Mustafa's tricks.

"'Travelers intending to cross the desert rest at Lop for a week to gather strength and arrange for guides and beasts,' Marco began. 'They have beautiful gardens there with pink and white oleander, rose laurel, and rushes. The afternoon we arrived they gave us sweet dates and strips of dried melon that tasted like honey. For supper we ate roast goat, lentils, spinach, and small cakes of nut paste pounded with honey.'

"Marco's mouth watered as he described the foods of Lop. He'd feasted there; remembering and telling of them made him hungry. His telling made Kublai hungry too. The emperor clapped his hands. Servants came with skewers of roasted lamb, a silver cup of koumiss, hot loaves of flatbread topped with honey, slices of apple and orange.

"The young man fell silent as the fragrance of roast meat, oranges, and baked bread filled the room.

"The emperor glared. 'Continue!' he mumbled through a full mouth.

"Marco said, 'I'm hungry too.'

" 'Speak!' Kublai yelled, meat crumbs and spit flying.

" 'A dry streambed makes no sound,' Marco replied.

"Kublai choked. For a long moment he looked at the Venetian as if he couldn't quite make him out. Then, puckering out his lips so the purple showed, he wagged his head from side to side, leaned back, and clapped again.

" 'For him,' he ordered when the servants came. 'Provide for this dry streambed so it may continue to sing until I slice off its head.' "

Mark grinned and pumped his fist in triumph.

"The servants were surprised," the doctor continued. "Only the highest officials were invited to eat with Kublai, and they had to eat standing up and wrap their mouths and noses in veils of silk embroidered with gold so their smell and breath would not come to Kublai's food. They had to cover their mouths with those napkins, too, when they giggled nervously at any joke the emperor made. Kublai himself rarely laughed. Angered or amused, he usually squinted, puffed out his lips, and wagged his head a little.

"When the servants brought Marco his napkin, he spread it in his lap. He never covered his mouth like the others did, and every plate the servers offered he seized and kept. Squatting on the thickest carpet, with knife and fingers he ate an emperor's meal: roasted nuggets of lamb, yogurt mixed with honey, saucer-shaped loaves of bread touched with salt. He washed his dinner down with a cup of koumiss.

"The koumiss warmed him. Kublai downed four cups. He was easier to deal with after his koumiss. He and his lieutenants drank little water; they drank koumiss all day long. On the steppes the wild horsemen offering koumiss to a guest would assist him in drinking by pulling his ears with great force to open his throat wider."

Mark cut in. "Sounds like they were drunk all the time!"

"Maybe," Hornaday said.

"Kublai kept making all these threats," Mark said. "Would he really kill Marco?"

"Maybe," said the doctor. "Who would stop him?"

"Marco's father and uncle?" Mark suggested.

Hornaday shook his head. "They weren't even allowed in the tent, and, anyway, they had no authority. Marco was on his own."

Hornaday continued with the story. "'So, Venetian,' Kublai bellowed as Marco wiped his lips, 'are you strong enough to speak again?'

"'Yes, Excellency. Thank you,' the young man said with a burp.

" 'Then do so!' Kublai roared with so much fury his guards reached for their curved knives.

"Marco cleared his throat and spat on the floor as Mustafa had instructed him. Mongols spat a lot, but again the guards were startled, because in Kublai's tent it was the custom that visitors carried a small vase for spitting so as not to soil the handsome carpets of silk and velvet.

" 'Many in the desert are diseased in the eyes,' Marco began, 'from exposure to the constant sun and the fine dust of the desert, or perhaps from the bites of flies that attack the eyes at all hours. The pupil goes cloudy; then the ball becomes like white stone. The women paint around their eyes to prevent the flies' biting. The men smear on a paste of minerals and oil.

" 'We treated them with an ointment we got in Syria. Some were helped, but none that had lost sight. I brought you a jar, Sire.'

"Kublai opened the jar. Inside was an odorless oily white cream.

" 'How do you use this?' he asked.

" 'You smear a small bit on the affected place. It soothes.'

" 'Do you know the secret of it?'

" 'What do you mean, Excellency?'

" 'Can you make it?'

"Marco shook his head. 'The apothecaries in Syria take a rare mineral quarried in the mountains and roast it in the hottest fire they can make. From the ash remaining they prepare this white material, which they mix with rarefied sheep tallow. They call it *tutty.* That is all I know.'

" 'Hah!' spat Kublai. 'You lie! You are saving the secret of it for your doctors in Venice. You will show us the trick of making it,' he said grimly. 'I will order a hundred of our Chinese who are trained in the healing arts to examine this and make the same. They will test it on you! Now resume your travels,' he growled.

"Marco clenched his teeth and swallowed hard.

" 'Cotton grows at Lop, Excellency,' he said. 'It is the best material for desert garb. There are fields of bushes blooming balls of that rare wool. Behind the low boundary walls of sundried clay there are also palm and vegetable gardens, orchards, and flowers.

" 'At the edge of the desert they have made it green with water led for miles from the Flame Hills in tiled tunnels that look like mounds flung up by gigantic moles. Where the land flattens out, the water is led to the fields and orchards in lined channels laid under the ground. One channel may have two hundred openings.

" 'Everything around is barren, but where the pipes serve, they grow onions, carrots, and spinach. For fruit they have date palms, figs, sweet apples, and white grapes the size of mare tits, which they dry into raisins and send off for trade by the hundredweight on the camel caravans. Their great delicacy, though, they save for themselves: tiny green raisins, green as grass, Sire—these,' he said, handing the emperor a small cotton sack filled with tiny green fruits bright as jewels.

"Kublai reached out eagerly. He emptied the sack into his palm and began to gobble the raisins in clots, nodding as he chewed.

" 'More!' he mumbled. 'More!'

" 'Through those tunnels,' Marco continued, 'they water fields of cotton for the fine white fibers they spin and weave into cloths like this, Sire,' he said, handing Kublai a square of brown, scarlet, and green. 'Those are the colors of that place.'

"Kublai had a palace full of such things, but it pleased him that the Venetian had thought to bring him a sample. He smiled.

"Marco saw his opportunity. 'Please, Sire, answer the question I put to you when I arrived: why do you with your thousands on thousands, as you said, demand of us a hundred of our teachers?'

"Kublai sat back. 'You ask the question my oldest

son should ask,' he murmured more to himself than to Marco.

"'Because you can conquer on horseback,' he replied, 'but you cannot rule on horseback. Would there have been a Roman Empire without mortar? You need the discipline of shared belief to bind people together. You can force them to submit with a large army, but every time the army moves away, there will be rebels and revolutions. What is required is a force greater than arms. There is no force greater than belief.

"'Consider, Venetian: it takes five soldiers to contain one rebel. Who are the pope's warriors? Monks. What are their weapons? Belief. The Buddhists have monks and beliefs, but they do not care about this world. They are like birds—they take what they find, and if they do not find, they go away. As for the followers of Islam, they make terrible subjects! They are all rebels! Even among themselves they fight. You go to any Arab village and ask the first person you meet, "Who is chief here?" and what will he answer? "Me!"

"'Your people are held together by the pope's single faith. However he manages it—through fear and hope—it works. Maybe Christianity is the mortar I need. Your priest teachers—if they ever arrive!—will debate the priests of the many religions here and perhaps show us a better way, teaching our people the orderly faithful habits they have taught the pope's many different tribes so all of ours will behave as one like his.

" 'So now, Impertinence, get on with your story of crossing the desert.'

" 'Not yet,' said Marco. 'How is it you are ruler here?'

" 'Because I am the strongest,' Kublai roared, seizing his heavy blade. 'With this I crush my rivals!' he said as he waved it over Marco's head.

" 'When my cousin set the people of his region against me, I attacked like lightning. We came five thousand strong on a nine days' march we made in three without stop.

" 'I rode to battle in a wooden tower carried by four elephants clad in leather armor. My battle platform was filled with crossbowmen, archers, and experts with the catapult and slingshot. Above us flew my banner of the sun and moon carried so high it could be seen on every side.

" 'I had gathered my troop in secret. I surprised my cousin, who had supposed my force much smaller.

" 'When all were lined up for battle, I sent my court jugglers, clowns, and acrobats forward with the musicians as we all began singing at the greatest pitch of our voices, for I had learned, Venetian, that a man who sings does not know fear.

"'So my troop marched forward, blind to fear and blind to the bodies of our slaughtered musicians and those others.

"'When I had won, I had my rival rolled up tight in a carpet and stomped by my elephants so the blood of the imperial Mongol lineage might not be spilled upon the earth. He was, after all, my cousin.'

"'Do many rebel now?' Marco wanted to know.

"'No,' the emperor replied. 'Unless things get very bad, people obey because they fear change. For most people, anything is better than change. They prefer the evil they know.'

"Marco nodded slowly. 'I have another question, Sire. What does it mean to rule?'

"Kublai laughed. 'I see your mind now! You plan to become a ruler!'

"'No,' said Marco. 'I just want to know what it means to rule.'

"Kublai was silent for a moment. When he started to speak, he looked away.

"'It means having everything and nothing,' he said. 'It means to be hungry in the presence of food, poor in the presence of wealth, lonely in the presence of people, weak in possession of power. Nothing belongs to the ruler. He owns and acts for his people, giving them what they cannot provide themselves: order above all.

" 'I've been in places where there was no order,' he said. 'They were dangerous. I don't ever want to go back to those places. There's no liberty without order, no happiness. In a free-for-all no man is free, not even the strongest.

" 'The ruler must strive to give his people security in their persons and property; then shelter, food, and water, and finally justice.

" 'Rebellions will happen, foreign armies will attack, wells will fail, locusts and blight will destroy crops—those are things the ruler must do his best to prevent or alleviate, but it is not always in his power to do so. It is always in his power to give justice.

" 'In the end, after order, being heard and getting justice are what matter most to people. When I send out spies and interrogate prisoners taken in war, the first question I ask is, "Where you come from, do you get justice?" No state lasts long where the people do not think so.'

"Kublai fell silent.

"Marco asked, 'What is your justice, Emperor?'

" 'Everywhere it is the same, Venetian: the fair distribution of whatever goods there are and prompt delivery of fair punishments.

" 'Now! Enough of this!' the great man exclaimed.

" 'Please, Sire,' said Marco, 'just one thing more. What is your most difficult task?'

"Kublai half closed his eyes. 'To listen. An old Jew merchant from Egypt told me the story of Solomon's dream when he became king. His god came offering to grant one wish. What did Solomon ask for? "Give me a listening heart to govern my people that I might make out between good and evil." Listening is my most difficult task.'

" 'Thank you,' Marco said with a bow.

"The hint of a smile crossed Kublai's face. He was becoming fond of this foreigner he called Impertinence, and Marco was becoming fond of him. Kublai paid Marco more attention than his father ever had. But he kept the young Venetian prisoner."

Dad,

Doc told me some Marco Polo stories that aren't in the book. I think he's guessing and making up a lot, but I don't care. I miss you a lot. Mom keeps saying you're OK and we're going to hear from you soon, but I'm not so sure. I hope so.

Love, Mark

18

The Wonders of China

Dusk was gathering on Christmas Eve. There were wisps of Christmas music in the air, along with the smells of good things cooking. The calle was bright with bustling people, shop lights, and excited chatter.

The signora put tall white candles on the tables. For the next two hours she rushed to serve the holiday crowd. Gradually the café emptied as folks headed home to dress for church.

The signora brought coffees and sat down heavily, legs out. "So what does Marco Polo do tonight?" she asked.

"Shegazhou sei!" the doctor shouted as he leaped up.

Boss barked and the signora screamed.

"That's what the guards would yell when Kublai approached," Hornaday said. "It means 'All go down.'

Everyone in earshot would fall to the ground, even the old and crippled. If you didn't, or you didn't go flat enough, the guards would poke you with their spears.

"Marco never did. He and Kublai's priest and the members of the high court were the only ones who didn't.

"Part of Kublai's genius was his ability to pick good people—men and women—to help him govern. Force alone will do for a while," the doctor said. "If you're the strongest, you can slaughter your opponents to get your way. In the long run, though, you need to rely on others. Bright people didn't threaten Kublai: he made them his own. Recognizing that some of his newly conquered Chinese subjects were better tax collectors, astronomers, record-keepers, and planners than his Mongol knights, he gave the Chinese high posts in his government.

"Kublai's religion relied on almanacs to predict the equinoxes, solstices, and celestial events. The best astronomers were Arabs, so Kublai hired those he could and bought others as slaves. They were all treated well. In his shops at Beijing his astronomers made instruments to study the skies, along with compasses, globes of bronze, and maps of the world as they knew it—Europe a blur, no New World, because Columbus wouldn't sail for two hundred years, and when he did, it was because Marco's book inspired him to go East.

"After a few weeks of questioning and listening to Marco, Kublai figured he could use the Venetian despite his ignorance of things Oriental.

"At first he had Marco report on what was going on in nearby villages and towns. The emperor said he wanted facts and numbers, but that's not what he sent Marco out for. He wanted stories about life. As much as he wanted to know what wealth his people had in metal and grain and what they needed by way of bridges and teachers, he was more eager to learn about their enchantments. The sight of a tiny golden Tibetan prayer drum on its stick with stones on strings to make it spin when you whirled it charmed him as much as a sack of pearls.

"Kublai had bragged to Marco about the thousand agents in his service—all those ears, eyes, tongues, and memories at his command. Not one of those thousands had Marco's eye for noticing or his tongue for telling.

"Marco looked closely and listened with his eyes shut to catch the smallest sound. He sniffed and touched and tasted to tell Kublai flavors and textures. He told how things felt. Both Marco and Kublai were hungry for the *feel* of things.

"Marco would never become Mongol; Kublai would never become European; yet for all their differences, their minds worked in the same way—fascinated by all manner of experience, ingenuity, and invention. Although Kublai had the mind of a ruler and Marco the mind of a merchant, they were alike in this: both were skeptical and tribal."

"Skeptical and tribal, Doc?" Mark asked. "What do you mean?"

"I mean they trusted only their own," the doctor replied. "They would use others, but for secrets and things of great importance, they used only those of their own blood.

"Marco's genius was to notice and then give the small details that tell the whole—the color in the mountain girl's cheeks as she sang her tribal song in a voice that seemed double, coming at once from her throat and her nose. He described for the old emperor the fullness of her lips, the scent of her hair. In his telling he captured the small pleasures that drifted and caught the light for an instant, then fell away like a feather from a passing bird.

"He went everywhere with a pointed stick of hard charcoal and small squares of paper to catch the stories he heard and novelties that struck him. Stories and strangenesses are like falling feathers—they pass and are gone forever unless you catch them as they go.

"When something struck Marco, he'd write a single word or draw a small sketch. To remember music he'd write the melody in musical notation with dots, bars, and slashes, the dots going up and down to show the tone on a scale, the slashes to indicate the rhythm.

"With these thumb-sized pages Marco could recall what he'd heard, seen, smelled, and tasted. He could describe in ways that surprised. When he told about the women watering their dooryard flowers in the evening, you felt the softness of the petals and smelled the vapors rising from the still-warm steps mixed with the fragrance of rose. In his telling you could hear the dry soil suck the moisture.

"What interested Marco interested Kublai—how at such and such a place far from the sea white cowrie shells from the Indian coast pass for money, while in another place, where salt is precious, small bricks of it stamped with the king's seal are exchanged for necessaries. He told what people in remote lands do with their dead—whether the bodies are buried and with what ceremony, or how the corpse is left on a platform of sticks to rot and be eaten by birds.

"In India, he reported, they burn their dead after a

great procession led by all the musicians in the village drumming and playing as loud as they can as they bear the body from its home to a pile of fragrant wood the family has paid a great sum for and placed in the road. This pyre is draped with silk and cloth of gold.

"When they are about to set it on fire, the mourners come to drink wine and make gifts of images cut out of paper representing slaves, horses, camels, and pieces of money, so in the next world the dead person will have slaves and beasts and coins. They call these paper coins magic money and give them to distressed travelers who are grateful to get them.

"He told the emperor what his far-off subjects wore and how much labor they had to give for it; how the people fixed their hair; what jewels they wore in their ears; what drugs they used for stimulants, stupor, and illness; and, most carefully, their perfumes, pleasures, and rituals, since those interested Kublai more than anything.

"Marco learned that Kublai had walled off part of the palace grounds for a garden he made and tended himself without help from anyone after his engineers had dug the pond and the royal elephants brought in the beautiful trees of that region with all the roots and much earth. In this most private place, the emperor grew fragrant roses and peonies and raised melons and pears for his own table. The walls were sealed save for one small door. Only he went in.

"The idea that Kublai kept a secret garden fascinated Marco. He'd had no experience with gardens—there were few of any size in Venice—but he imagined a new way of pleasing the emperor. On a trip through the northern mountains, he collected bulbs of the fragrant lily that blooms there and roots of the small shrub azalea with intricate pink flowers and honey scent.

"He said nothing as he carried these into Kublai's tent.

"That afternoon Marco became the first outsider to be admitted to the emperor's private garden. On every trip thereafter he collected plants.

"Kublai's empire included Buddhists, Hindus, Christians, Muslims, a few Jews, pagans, and followers of innumerable cults. Kublai tolerated them all. 'We Mongols believe that there is only one God,' he told Marco one afternoon, 'but as God gives us the different fingers of the hand, so he gives to men diverse ways of understanding and believing in Him.'

"The emperor's own spiritual adviser was the filthily robed, strange-eyed priest who read the cracks in baked bones of sacrificed animals for messages from Kublai's ancestors. He would bring Kublai these chalk white bones and tell him the portents he read in the fine gray tracery of cracks through his one bulging eye as the other wambled heavenward.

"This man knew the rare breathing art that enabled him to generate body heat to keep warm while he slept naked on a bare stone bed in a cold room.

"Because Kublai was anxious to keep on good terms with his ancestors, this priest was, after the emperor, the most powerful person at court. In addition to reading the ancestors' news in the burned bones, this man claimed to control the weather over the imperial palace. He never said what it was going to be but claimed to have made it what it was.

"The priest grew suspicious of Marco's influence. He ordered Kublai to summon Marco to explain his faith, 'for that is the doorway to his inner mind,' he said.

"Marco came as ordered. The strange-eyed shaman stood silent, his dark orange robe torn and spotted, his hair unkempt under his flat hat made of red fox paws. He smelled stale.

" 'Explain your faith, Venetian,' Kublai ordered in a dry voice.

"Marco was at a loss. He knew the rites and rituals of his church, he could recite the creed and the prayers, but to say what his faith was?

"His hands went cold. Mustafa had not prepared him for this.

"The two men waited.

"Kublai's stare did not unsettle him so much as the old priest's eyes, for with the one he would squint; then he'd bend down holding his hat to tilt his head so the other could take him in.

"Then Marco remembered a lesson he'd heard as a boy.

" 'Late one winter afternoon,' he said in a voice so soft Kublai and the priest had to lean forward to hear, 'a sparrow slipped into a warm room through a crack, flitted across, then flew out again into winter darkness. So the life of man appears to me, Sire, here for a little season, but of what follows or what has gone before we have no idea. My faith is that by following the law of Christ, our prophet, there is hope of continuing warm. For that hope I believe His law is worthy to be followed.'

"The priest had closed his eyes. Kublai sat silent for a long moment.

" 'When you arrived,' Kublai said at last, 'I asked you what you missed most of your home. You spoke of sounds. Today I ask you for your faith and you speak of hope. There is no substance to those things.'

"He shook his head. 'Go. Bring news. Bring me a remedy for the pain that burns my joints.'

"Despite his fear, by now Marco had come to love the old man," the doctor continued, "so everywhere he went, he hunted for medicines, but for what Kublai suffered, there was no cure."

Mark glanced at the doctor's hands.

Hornaday noticed and shrugged. "Every time Marco returned from a trip," he went on, "he'd report on wars in neighboring lands, rulers overthrown, armies in revolt, civil war, and tell the stories he'd heard there. Kublai usually knew the news and he must have known some of the stories too, but he loved hearing Marco tell them.

"Returning from one assignment, Marco told Kublai about the caliph of Baghdad, who had raided and robbed his neighbors to get up a huge pile of gold. 'Everyone around knew how greedy he was,' Marco reported, 'and how brutal. There were plots to overthrow him, but the caliph had a large army and the city walls were strong. He sat fat and safe on a thick pile of rare carpets.

" 'Then a man even greedier heard about him.

" 'This man, a general named Hulegu, got all the secrets about the strength and wealth of Baghdad.

" 'Hulegu figured he couldn't beat the caliph's army head-on, so he planned a trick.

" 'He marched his troops toward Baghdad faster than word of them could travel, wiping out all the outlying garrisons and towns that might send warning.

" 'While still miles away from the great walled city, he divided his force into three parts. He hid one part in the woods by the river Tigris, spreading them out behind trees, in the tall grass, and in trenches they dug and then covered over with dirt, leaves, and branches.

" 'The second part he had bury itself in the weeds and mud of the marsh wilds beyond the river.

" 'When morning came, Hulegu marched what looked like a puny pretend army toward the great bronze gates of Baghdad, banners flying, kettle drums booming, battle horns dinning.

" 'Hulegu had his bagpipers out front bleating their strange music while he followed behind, unarmed and bareheaded on his great white horse. He wore a vest of glittering gold chain. His men wore helmets of shined copper decorated with wooden beaks, eagle feathers, and painted eyes so they looked like the heads of monster birds. The horses wore greased leather battle aprons that looked like sheets of oiled metal.

" 'The caliph was surprised, but the attacking force was small, so he was not frightened. He sneered at his enemy's strange helmets. He laughed as he unfurled his banner of Muhammad and rode out to destroy them.

" 'Those helmets, though, and the bagpipes, scared his soldiers, and when their horses sniffed the breeze, they turned skittish.

蒂姆

"'Hulegu had ordered his horses' battle aprons smeared with stinking rancid yak butter and the powerful dung of that animal. The smell was nothing to his mounts—they'd been trained to it—but it spooked the caliph's, which knew nothing of yaks.

"'Even so, the caliph's captains ordered their men forward, screaming over their fear, whipping their horses until blood dripped.

"'As the caliph's men approached, Hulegu's force scattered, swirling away like a flock of starlings, then gathering and aiming toward their hidden comrades.

"'Once the caliph's men entered into the trap, Hulegu's soldiers rose up on all sides, banging boards together to sound like many more than they were.

"'Confused and terrified, the caliph's men were slaughtered, he was captured, Baghdad taken.

"'Hulegu went to the treasure tower. There was even more gold than rumored.

"'He ordered the caliph brought before him.

"'"Caliph," he said, "why have you heaped up all this gold? Why didn't you hire more knights to fight the likes of me?"

"'The caliph spat and said nothing.

"'"So," said Hulegu, nodding slowly. "I see how it is with you. Well, since you love gold so much, I'll leave you your own to eat."

" 'He ordered the caliph sealed in his treasure tower, then called from the outside, "Caliph! Swallow all the gold you want! You will get nothing else!"

" 'The caliph was a big tubby man, but at the end of four days he was dead.'

"Kublai nodded slowly when Marco finished. 'I know that story,' he said.

"Marco blushed. 'Forgive me, Sire,' he said, 'but why did you allow me to tell you something you already knew?'

" 'To test your care,' the old man replied. 'A story is like a bowshot. The bow must be taut, the arrow straight, and the aim true, or the point goes to nothing. You did well.'

"No praise ever meant more to Marco."

Mark nodded. He knew how he'd feel if he ever heard the words "You did well" from his dad.

19

THE PLOT

"The emperor began sending Marco farther and farther afield," the doctor continued, "one stint to inspect the wild regions of Tibet, another to Burma and India and back by sea. Some of those trips took years.

"'So, Venetian!' Kublai would bark in his high voice when Marco returned. 'Speak! Empty your head to me or I will cut it off!'

"'At such a place,' Marco reported after one trip, 'the Golden King's lieutenants decorate their upper arms by taking a cluster of sharp quills tied together and stabbing their own flesh until the blood comes. They rub the wound with grains of a soft black stone found there. If the wound does not infect, the design lasts like a scar and is borne as a jewel. For some, though, the black grains act as a slow poison and they die. This is taken as proof that they were unworthy of the ornament.

" 'There are huge serpents at that place,' he said, 'lizards ten paces in length and in bulk as big around as a vinegar cask. They have two clawed forelegs near the head, and the mouth is big enough to swallow a man whole. Their eyes rise in horny lumps off the snout like loaves of bread.

" 'These serpents are creatures of custom. They follow the same muddy trails from water hole to water hole. The hunters take them by planting blades of sharpened bamboo in the steep ruts they follow, so as the crocodile slithers along and begins his slide into the water, he slits himself from throat to tail.

" 'The huntsmen extract its gall and sell it for a great price as medicine against the bite of a mad dog, cure for the itch, and remedy for sore joints.

" 'I brought you some, Excellency,' Marco said, handing over a tube made of bamboo.

"Kublai lifted the pelts that covered his swollen ankles and rubbed on the salve.

" 'Yesterday,' the old man muttered, 'the fifty witches sent by the king of Chosen—Korea—came here in their stinking fish-skin boots to cure me with their sacred chickens. They danced and shouted and wrung chicken necks until the air filled with blood and feathers and the women fell down senseless.

"'I hope your medicine serves me better! I sent them off with a curse, but if your remedy fails . . .'

"He paused and narrowed his eyes. 'As it will . . .'

"Marco bowed low.

"Kublai laughed. 'Stand up, Venetian. Bowing does not become you.'

"Returning from another trip, Marco said, 'My lord, the mountain people at such a place do not swim, and they do not know about boats. When they come to a deep river, they sew skins together to hold their goods, tie the bundles to their horses' tails, mount, and let the horses swim them across.

"'They use no water for bathing, believing it a sin to corrupt water with the filth of the body. To clean themselves they have their slaves scald their skins with hot scented oil and scrape their bodies all over just as we scrape a hide to take off the hair. So they remove whatever hair they have, for they consider such hair unsightly, even their eyebrows.'

"'Did you allow yourself to be washed in their manner?' Kublai asked.

"'I did, Sire. I suffered blisters and many cuts. My skin burned for weeks after, and I smelled evil to myself, but the people smiled and said it made me handsome and pleasant of aroma—as handsome and pleasant, they said, as one of my color might be, for my color and body smell they found offensive.

"'After dinner their chief and his women danced to horns and a rhythm of tambourines and drums—like this, Sire,' Marco said, taking a small tambourine from his coat and rattling and thumping it as he shuffled the steps he'd seen, until Kublai began to sway slightly on his throne as he imagined those women weaving to the wail of horns and the thrum of drums and tambourines.

"'Coming out of those mountains, Emperor, I entered a world of yellow haze—dust of the plains carried on the winds like smoke. The people there say it is not unusual for the air to be hazy in that way for months at a time. Only when the rains come does it go away. Many suffer from breathing it, Sire, and it hurts the eyes. The farmers say it is their best soil blowing into the next world.' "

The doctor paused.

"As you might imagine, some of the emperor's Mongol barons grew jealous of the attention Kublai paid Marco and the gifts he gave him—embroidered silks, rubies, peacock feathers, pots of musk—that otherwise might have gone to them.

"At first they said to one another, 'Never mind, he will soon run out of stories, and then the emperor will tire of him.' But two months, a year, two, and still

Marco held Kublai's attention, sometimes for as much as an hour after he met with his clerks and the petitioners in the morning.

"'He is taking what belongs to us,' the jealous ones whispered to one another.

"A small group of those people conspired to poison Marco with something slow—a poison added to his salt.

"Kublai read their minds. He knew they were jealous. He mistrusted the Venetian too—he mistrusted everyone. That's the way it is with rulers: they set spies to watch their spies. Kublai paid his spies well and made sure they were unaware of each other.

"The emperor had assigned spies to watch Marco—to follow him, report on him, protect him, taste his food before it reached his lips, do what he did. More than one of them collapsed trying to keep up with Marco. The agent who suffered the bath of hot oil with him died.

"The conspirators bribed one of those spies to bring them any news that might discredit the Venetian. From him they learned about Marco's practice of carrying small squares of paper everywhere and stopping as he traveled to fill them with marks and tiny sketches.

"They ordered the bribed spy to bring them some of those notes. Using his seal of authority, this man entered

Marco's chambers in the imperial guest suite and stole a few of the squares.

"At first the conspirators couldn't make anything of them. 'It's a secret Venetian code,' they agreed, 'but what's it about?' They puzzled for days over his marks. Then they came upon the ones with marks and dashes. These got them excited like a hive of stirred-up wasps. They paced around the table where they had some of Marco's strips laid out, fiddling and rearranging, trying to make something of the strange patterns.

"Suddenly the youngest of them, the one they called No Mouth because his nose seemed to meet his chin, cried out that he'd broken the code.

" 'It's a map of our armies,' he said, pointing to the

squares with dots and dashes he'd arranged like the boundary of Kublai's domain.

"'Each dot stands for a place; the dashes show the troop strengths.'

"Smirking, giggling, chortling, and hugging one another, the conspirators toasted No Mouth with cups of rice wine. 'We've got him!' they exclaimed. 'Here is treason! Everything Kublai has given to him will be distributed to us.'

"They hurried to Kublai. 'He is a spy, a traitor,' No Mouth exclaimed as he showed the emperor the squares of paper.

"'Are there more?' Kublai demanded.

"'Many, Sire.'

"'Gather them all.'

"The spy was sent back to Marco's room. He took all the squares he could find.

"The chief conspirator presented them to Kublai.

"The emperor summoned Marco.

"'So, Venetian,' said Kublai in a strange voice, 'these people have shown me your maps and notes of stolen secrets.'

"Kublai picked up one of the slips.

"'Reveal your secret, traitor,' he hissed.

"The conspirators, sure they had their man, grinned and shuffled with excitement.

"Slowly Kublai turned to look at them. There was something in his look that froze them. Spittle began dribbling down No Mouth's chin.

"Kublai turned to Marco. 'Reveal the secret in this one,' he ordered. 'These dots up and down, these dashes and slash marks—that man there says this is a map showing the locations of our armies. Explain, Venetian!'

"Marco studied the slip and began to sing the chant music of Tibet.

"As Kublai's priest listened, his odd eyes rolled and wandered. He recognized the music. How did Marco learn it? he wondered. How did he remember it?

"'And this one?' Kublai demanded, pushing another square of paper at Marco.

"Again the Venetian sang, a different song this time. And so it went, through all the chants and songs Marco had sung to Kublai, for it was the song slips the conspirators had taken as proof of Marco's treachery.

"'So,' said the emperor, turning to the assembled plotters at last. 'Who else schemed to rid me of the Venetian? Who told you he was taking bribes and selling secrets?'

"They held themselves motionless, silent as stones.

"'Very well,' he said with a thin smile. 'You know my ways of finding out.'

"No one heard their screams, but the next afternoon when Marco entered the white tent, he saw fresh blood and hair on Kublai's sword.

"Although the old priest had known of the plot, he was spared, because he told Kublai the ancestors had predicted everything.

"He was waiting in his filthy robes and fox-paw hat when Marco returned to Kublai's tent. He gave the Venetian an evil look with his bulging eye. His hands shaped the tying of a knot.

"It was the sign for 'You are next.'

"A shiver went through Marco."

Mark shivered too.

20

Escape!

Mark's mother rose from the table, pointing to the guttering candles.

"Everyone's left," she said. "We're keeping the signora. She must dress for church—the midnight Mass."

"No, wait," said Mark. "How did Marco get away?"

"Please, how?" asked the signora. "If I do not hear, I do not sleep. I go to Mass tomorrow."

Mark's mother sat down. "How *did* Marco escape?" she asked.

"Luck," said the doctor. "Every time Marco mentioned his desire to go home, the Great Khan's face would grow terrible and he'd make a dark noise. The Polos understood that without the emperor's permission they'd never be able to leave. They were free to travel, but only within Kublai's domain. They were watched. Kublai's men knew everything about them.

"The Polos had been in Kublai's court for almost twenty years. The emperor was nearing eighty. They were anxious to get out before he died, because they knew the Mongol custom: those who were close to the dead ruler, especially foreigners, were executed by people loyal to his successor.

"When a ruler died, every person who happened to encounter his funeral procession was put to the sword. 'Go!' the cortege attendants would cry. 'Serve your lord in the next world!'

"So the Polos drifted toward a sure and grisly end until the night a squad of post riders accompanying three royal messengers from Tabriz came ringing bells and blowing trumpets as their horses thundered through the palace gates.

"The messengers were filthy, their faces cracked, eyes bloodshot and sunken, their bodies ravaged. They'd ridden for weeks, resting not more than four hours in twenty-four, to bring news that the wife of Kublai's cousin at Tabriz had died in childbirth. In her last breath she'd begged her husband to marry quickly another of the same Mongol family because he was growing old and needed an heir.

"Kublai was fond of this kinsman. He ordered his wives to select the most promising young noblewoman of his court to be the bride.

"It was the way of things that the girl was not asked if she wished to marry a man three times her age who lived half a continent away. She would be told of the great honor bestowed on her and that would be that.

"It wasn't long before Kublai's four wives had selected a girl of the imperial Mongol blood. Kublai met her and agreed.

"Morning Flower was seventeen, finely shaped, skilled in music and dance. She could paint hundreds of Chinese characters perfectly with the black ink brush. 'She has sweet breath and is without blemish,' the women reported. 'And she does not snore.'

"But how to get her safely from Kublai's winter capital at Khanbaliq—present-day Beijing—to Tabriz? The distance was more than five thousand miles by the Road of Silk with its twistings of unpaved track and the ups and downs of the mountain crossings.

"The road was all trouble," Hornaday continued. "Every day the emperor got news of bandits, wars, storms, floods, washed-out bridges, landslides. The princess was not told how dangerous the journey would be. She had fears and sadness enough on leaving everything and everyone she'd ever known to be the wife to a stranger who did not even speak her language.

"Her maids and attendants, too, set out in ignorance, but not the six hundred soldiers in her entourage. They'd heard rumors about what they faced. Despite the gallons of koumiss, the thousand flags, the fireworks, gongs, drums, and trumpets celebrating the princess's departure, her soldiers were sullen.

"News of the rich travelers sped ahead of them. The storms they met, the washed-out bridges and bad roads were nothing compared to the armies of bandits that picked off her scouts and rearguard troops and made desperate sallies to carry off the princess herself and her treasure.

"Often they attacked at night, shooting fire arrows into the royal camp and making terrible noises to frighten the animals. Twice they attacked in daylight, clad in white tunics and screaming like wolves at the moment the sun was drilling into the eyes of her defenders. Many of her people were lost, but the captains urged the caravan on. They knew they faced death at Kublai's hand if they turned back.

"They crept westward, some days accomplishing only ten miles. They fell behind their plan to clear before winter the mountains where Marco had fallen sick.

"The snows caught them. Many of their beasts died. Soldiers and some of the royal attendants suffered frostbite, chunks of cheek falling away, fingers and toes turning black and rotting. Still they pressed on. Then one morning the captains were found murdered. That day the party turned back.

"They'd traveled for more than a year. When the survivors reported to Kublai what they'd suffered, he decided to send the princess and her retinue by sea from China to Hormuz.

"Her convoy would sail down the east coast of China, pass through the Strait of Malacca—notorious for pirates—cross the Bay of Bengal, travel north up the coast of India, cross the Arabian Sea, and sail up the Persian Gulf to Hormuz.

"Marco and his dog had just sailed much of that route. The princess's people begged Kublai to let them have him for a guide.

" 'We are Mongols,' they pleaded, 'we are strangers to navigation. The ship captains are Chinese, the navigators are Arab: we do not trust any of them. They will sell us to the pirates. Only Marco can protect us. He knows how to follow the route by the stars, so he can tell if we are going the right way.'

"Kublai did not want to let Marco go, but he didn't want to offend his kinsman either.

"Chinese merchant ships were huge, the largest in the world, some with as many as four masts and twelve sails. They had deck cabins for passengers and crews of three hundred. Kublai ordered thirteen of these fitted and provisioned for a voyage of two years.

"Each vessel carried immense cedar vats of fresh water, rice stored in sealed clay pots, tubs of sifted soil to grow fresh vegetables, coops of chickens, and flocks of goats for eggs, milk, and meat.

"Kublai saw the princess and the Polos off from his new palace at Beijing. His gout was too painful for him to travel with them to the coast.

"Morning Flower meant little to him. She'd come down from Mongolia to the Chinese capital for training three years before. The emperor hardly knew her, nor did he care about the elder Polos. Every day with no concern he sent off to risk of death men he was closer to.

"But Marco was different. Never again would he have a friend who pleased him so much and knew his heart so well.

"'Send word,' the old man said as he handed Marco the paiza, the slender strip of gold that would assure him safe passage, mounts, and provisions all the way to Tabriz.

"Kublai pinched his lips together. 'Return quickly,' he said in a husky voice.

"He turned away. He knew better than to ask for Marco's promise to return.

"Kublai hadn't thought it likely that the princess would find Marco handsome. He was, by Mongol standards, a curiosity: a person so strange as not to count in society, for he was European, poor, his smell was odd, and, most important, he was not of the blood imperial.

"Marco, though, might fall in love with the girl in the course of their long trip together, so Kublai arranged that the Venetian should never see her. Her land caravan would be closed; on shipboard she would be sequestered in a separate vessel. Everyone was under orders to assure her privacy.

"Until the royal flotilla entered the Bay of Bengal, Marco never did see her. Then a typhoon struck. Nine of the largest junks sank with all hands lost. The command ship carrying the princess and the senior officers of her retinue was battered beyond repair. They transferred to Marco's vessel.

"He was on deck when she came aboard. His heart went out to her, first in sympathy, then with something more. He would remember that moment the rest of his life. As an old man he carried in his heart the picture of her broad tan forehead, thick black hair, and steady dark eyes. A shadow of a smile had passed over her face when she'd noticed his dog."

Boss's tail thumped the floor.

Hornaday nodded and went on. "It turned out she was curious about the ways of Westerners, especially their odd writing. The only time Marco's hand touched hers was when he helped her shape the letters of his name in his language. She saved that paper."

Mark caught himself with cold hands shaping the letters of his own name.

"The shattered flotilla put in on the island of Sumatra, where they spent five months refitting and waiting out the typhoon season.

"Marco explored the island for foods and medicines, testing on some of the ailing sailors a palm elixir the natives said healed all ills. He brought the princess palm wine and palm sugar—things they had never known before. The wine was potent; they got giddy together. One afternoon they ate another new thing—pieces of coconut—and drank its sweet water.

"Once the worst of the storm season was past, they set out up the funnel-shaped Strait of Malacca, five hundred miles long, ten miles across at the narrow end, famous for *lanun*—pirates.

"They weren't many days under way before the

lanun fell upon them like a swarm of wasps. They'd heard about the rich flotilla refitting on Sumatra.

"It was the pirates' way to work together, picking off one vessel at a time, ramming, burning, slashing and screaming as they boarded, then stripping it and taking the sailors for slaves. Their secret weapon was a flaming concoction of naphtha and quicklime hurled by catapult at the victims' rigging.

"Another ship was lost. By the time they escaped the pirates and entered the Bay of Bengal, the princess's fleet was down to three.

"Storms continued to ravage the imperial flotilla, but disease was the greatest enemy now. Every day they pitched overboard victims of fever and the wasting sickness."

"What's wasting sickness, Doc?" Mark asked.

"Cholera—attacks of diarrhea so intense the body loses gallons of water in hours as the flesh shrinks back against the skull and blood turns to jelly."

Mark grimaced.

"Yes," said Hornaday, "and the doge had figured sea travel would be easier and safer than following the Road of Silk!

"Two years after the princess's great fleet set sail from China, three shaken vessels landed at Hormuz. Of the six hundred persons in the royal retinue, only the princess and seventeen of her people had survived.

"It was now Marco's responsibility to transport the girl overland to Tabriz. He needed pack animals, camels, and horses. Most important, he needed a suitable mount for the princess.

"Marco and the princess came upon a donkey in the bazaar, a large gray donkey with long broad ears and a habit of lying down unexpectedly. He was lying down when they passed by. The trader was kicking and whipping him with his switch. The donkey had large black eyes. He winced every time his master struck, but he would not move.

"The princess said she must have that animal. Suddenly that worthless, lazy, troublesome donkey became the most valuable one in the market.

"He had no name. He was plump, though; someone had cared for him before he fell on ill luck and ended up in the market. Perhaps his master—or mistress more likely—had died. Hormuz was an unhealthy place.

"The donkey had long expressive ears—big even for a donkey—long as a boy's arm and a palm wide, tough and muscular, well furred, always moving. He would bring them forward when pleased or expectant,

lower them when dejected, lay them back when angry. His short tail was twitchy and expressive too.

"Even with the princess on his back the donkey continued his habit of lying down without notice when fatigued or of a mind to rest. He'd wobble his front legs as a warning for the girl to dismount. If she didn't do so quickly, the donkey would fold his fronts and tumble the royal passenger over his head and go off for a nap.

"The princess's attendants were all for whipping him on, but she wouldn't allow it. She knew it wouldn't do any good anyway. When her donkey napped, the princess napped, and so did everyone else.

"The donkey had two brands on his left side, each as large as a hand. If those marks spelled a word, Marco couldn't make it out. No one else could either, so Marco named the donkey after his best friend at home, Mauricio. The way the princess pronounced it, it sounded like Ma-rick-o.

"When word of the royal party's arrival at Hormuz reached the court at Tabriz, a party of horsemen was sent out to escort them north. The commander brought news that the king whom the princess was to have married had died. Now she was to marry a younger relative of no great reputation. That meant she wouldn't become a queen after all. Instead, she'd become one of the harem wives—a lonely, unwanted exile in a mountain valley that looked nothing like the thick grassed steppes she'd known as a child or the rich smoky bustle of Kublai's imperial winter court at Beijing.

"She dreamed of going on to Venice with Marco, but she couldn't. She knew that if anyone had even guessed her dream, they would have killed him.

"As the entourage drew up at the court of her husband-to-be, Morning Flower dismounted. She kissed the donkey goodbye, bowed to Marco, then averted her face and turned weeping to her maids.

"As the gates crashed shut, someone slipped Marco a package—the headdress of a Mongol princess, adorned with gold, precious stones, and pearls. There was no note.

"The headdress was found among Marco's possessions after he died. No one in his family had ever seen it."

"Mom showed it to me in the museum," Mark blurted, "but they didn't say it was anything special. They didn't say it had belonged to the princess he took care of."

Hornaday shook his head slightly and took a deep breath.

"Later, back in Venice," he said, "Marco dreamed of putting on Tartar robes and returning to Tabriz with the golden pass and a forged letter from Kublai requesting permission for her to come visit. He imagined bringing lavish gifts of opium, pearls, and silk to her husband to show Kublai's respect.

"He wrote. She never answered. How could she? Whom could she trust with her letters?

"Then he heard that she'd died."

The doctor pinched his lips together and opened his hands. "That's it," he said.

Like the teacher you tried to save at Kirkuk, Mark thought.

The signora got up and gathered them all in a huddle. Nobody said anything.

Dad,

I wish you were here. I can't picture you in what Mom calls the ocean of sand. I wonder if the water problem makes you want to get away. At first we joked about your eating grilled goat and goat cheese, but maybe that's all there is, so it doesn't seem funny anymore. It's Christmas Eve here and this place is spooky. Most of the buildings are dark and the water is black. Mom says maybe there's stuff going on inside but I don't see any lights. It's like the people who lived there all died. If you were here, I'd show you the stone camel. It's cold here. I hope you are warm. I miss you a lot. Merry Christmas.

Love, Mark

21

Finding Marco

It was midnight when Mark and his mother got back to their hotel. All over Venice, bells were chiming and booming.

As Mark pushed open the hotel door, the clerk upstairs started yelling.

"All evening the person from the agency is been here! He have just left! He leave this for you," he said as they panted up the last steps.

He handed over a rumpled gray envelope covered with strange stamps. "Here is the man's number. He say call, no matter how late the time."

Smeared cancelation marks covered the writing, but Mark recognized the handwriting. "Mom!" he exclaimed. "It's from Dad!"

He tore open the envelope.

Dear Marian, dear Mark,

If I'm lucky, a nearly blind old man who calls himself Mustafa and says he's making a last visit to his home village will carry this letter to you to a pickup point five or six days' march from here. I'm coming home. I've got parasites. Nothing the locals have is touching them. Bad water. Many animals have died, and I've lost all my oomph. I'll come back someday to finish my work. Maybe Mark will come with me. "Postage" cost me my sovereigns.

See you soon!
All my love, Dad

"What a Christmas present!" Mark cried.

His mother was already on her phone, calling the agency chief at his home.

"They've found him!" she whispered to Mark as she listened. "They're going to fly him back to Baltimore day after tomorrow—the twenty-sixth. We'll fly back then too!"

As Mark got into bed and slipped the Chinese pillow under his head, he felt something at his feet. He groped around and came up with a small white cowrie shell.

There was a rustling in the corner.

"Good, you got it," Count Leo announced. "It

was Marco's good luck piece. You're the next in line, so you should have it."

"What do you mean I'm the next in line?" Mark asked.

"It's in your father's letter," Leo explained. "Next time he goes out, you're going too. So Merry Christmas and *tanti auguri,* as the locals say. Good luck!"

* * *

Christmas Day dawned bright and cold. Mark woke up to bells that rang like flights of soaring birds, wheeling and gathering to soar again.

It was sunny. A sharp breeze blew off the lagoon. The campo was filled with brightly dressed people waving and yelling to one another, *"Buon Natale!"* Somewhere close, trumpets were playing.

Hornaday and Boss met them at the café. As his mother told the doctor their great news, Mark hugged the dog hard. Boss switched his immense tail in pleasure and licked the boy's hand.

The café wasn't open, but the signora, just back from Mass, had hot milk, coffee, and biscotti for them. She looked different in a black dress and shiny new shoes. "For the Mass," she explained as she limped around. "Only for that do I put on these shoes."

As they finished breakfast, Hornaday leaned

back and looked at Mark. "Sooo," he drawled, "do you think there might be room back home in Baltimore for Boss?"

Mark wasn't sure he'd heard right. His eyes filled as he looked at the dog. Could Boss be *his*?

The doctor was nodding with a big smile and blinking hard.

Mark looked over at his mother. From the way she was smiling, he could tell she was in on it.

The dog was in on it too. As he looked up at Mark, he let out a long joyful howl.

"But won't you miss him, Doc?" Mark asked.

"I'll get along okay," the doctor said in a tight voice. "Venice is no place for a big dog like Boss, and I figure he and you need each other just like Marco needed his dog."

"Oh wow!" Mark said.

Before Mark could say thank you, Hornaday stood up, shook out his great white handkerchief, and rubbed his face hard.

"I have something else for you," he said as he handed Mark a small twist of red paper with an ivory carving of a rat inside. "Chinese," he explained. "After all, it's the Year of the Rat."

"Gee, Doc," said Mark. "It looks really old."

"Maybe it was Marco Polo's," said his mother, laughing.

"And this you already know about," the doctor added as he passed over the scimitar wrapped in his red wool scarf.

At the Christmas market Mark had gotten the signora a santon of a beaming woman in a white blouse and bright red peasant dress carrying a heaping bowl of dark yellow pasta. For his mother he'd found a maroon silk scarf decorated with Chinese letters in bold brushstrokes; for Hornaday, a wood carving of a black herding dog.

The doctor smiled in a strange way when Mark gave him the carving.

"For you," said the signora, holding out a CD. "The music you nod your head to here, Vivaldi. And this," she said, handing Mark a small carving of the Madonna. "So you will remember us at the café. Eh?"

Mark swallowed hard as a storm of feeling swept over him. He was close to crying.

"Th-thanks. Thank you all," he stammered.

The signora got up and hugged him.

They sat quietly together for several minutes. Then Mark looked closely at the figure the signora had just given him. "Yours has all that paint on her," he said, pointing. "Why?"

"She was a rescued," the signora replied. "I found her lying beside a wall. Someone did that bad thing to her, I don't know why, but she is safe here."

Suddenly Mark stood up. "Mom, Doc," he said,

"can we go back to Ca Polo the way we went the first time?"

"Sure, why not?" his mother said.

Mark went back to his room for the Marco Polo mask.

Just after they crossed the Rialto Bridge, he stopped. "Doc, do me a favor and go sit over there," he said, pointing to an empty box beside a mooring post.

"You want a picture?" the doctor asked.

"No. Just go sit on that box. Take off your hat."

Mark stepped back and squinted. Then he stepped back some more. The slanting winter light caught the bent-over head of the dark man.

"That's how he saw him the first time," Mark said. "He must have looked like that."

"Who?" his mother asked.

"Mustafa," Mark explained. "That's how Mustafa must have looked when Marco saw him the first time. He was Marco's teacher in the school of the street. He told Marco what to expect on the Road of Silk and how to act when he got to Kublai."

It was dusk by the time they reached Ca Polo.

Mark looked around the campo.

"Leave me here with Boss for a little while," he said. "We'll meet you over in that café."

Holding the Polo mask before his face, Mark waited with Boss in a corner of the square. The sky was like slate. It was damp and cold and absolutely still.

A shape appeared. A boy Mark's age came to the cistern with a bucket to get water.

Boss jerked up. Mark caught his breath.

"Yes," he whispered.

He couldn't make out the other boy's face, but he recognized the shape: it was like his own. The clothes were like those on the Polo figure in the museum.

"Ciao, Marco!" he called.

The other turned and stared, trying to make out the caller. Then he smiled and waved.

"Ciao, Marco!" he called back. *"Ciao, cane!" Hello, Marco! Hello, dog!*

Boss woofed.

Just then a window opened and a woman leaned out—*"Marco! Vieni qua!"* she hollered in a sharp voice. *Come here!*

The boy answered, "*Sì, Zia Anna. Sì! Vengo! Vengo!* Yes, Aunt Anna. I'm coming! I'm coming!" and he hurried off.

Slowly Mark and Boss walked to the café where the others were waiting. It was like a dream, but it wasn't a dream; they'd seen him! Mark was sure of it.

He fumbled in his pocket for the cowrie charm.

Suddenly he pictured himself sitting with his father at the kitchen table with the scale as they planned their Gobi trip. He was ready. He and Boss were ready to go exploring like Marco.

And he'd write about it.

Author's Note

From ear to ear the story has passed till it reached mine . . .

This is a fiction. The spine of travel is somewhat as Marco described it, as are the ribs of the larger adventures. The rest is imagined but possible, including my guess that Marco and his father and uncle were on a mission for the doge and that members of the Jewish merchant community in Venice helped them.

I've imagined the first time Marco told of his travels—his reports to Kublai—and their back-and-forth as the emperor came to appreciate His Impertinence. I have no proof, but I'm pretty sure Marco used notes for those reports and used them again when he told his story to Rustichello.

A compact and convenient edition of *The Travels* is

one edited by Manuel Komroff and published by the Modern Library, New York, 1926. I've worked from two longer versions, one edited by Henry Yule in 1871 and revised by Henri Cordier in 1903, republished by Dover in 1993, which from now on I'll refer to as "Y-C." It has excellent notes. The other, *Marco Polo: The Description of the World,* was edited by A. C. Moule and Paul Pelliot (London: G. Routledge, 1938), "M-P." Of the two, M-P is more readable, but it has few notes.

Another retelling I've used that has a lot of good background and some wonderful illustrations is Laurence Bergreen's *Marco Polo: From Venice to Xanadu* (New York: Alfred A. Knopf, 2007), "Bergreen."

For general background I read Colin Thubron's *Shadow of the Silk Road* (New York: HarperCollins, 2007), "Thubron"; Jean Bowie Shor's *After You, Marco Polo* (New York: McGraw-Hill Book Company, Inc., 1955), "Shor"; the 11th edition *Encyclopedia Britannica* essay "Marco Polo"; and Leonardo Olschki's *Marco Polo's Asia: An Introduction to His Description of the World,* translated by John A. Scott (Berkeley: University of California Press, 1960).

To add to what Marco Polo told about desert life and travel, I read T. E. Lawrence's *Revolt in the Desert* (London: Jonathan Cape, 1927), "Lawrence," and

Charles M. Doughty's *Travels in Arabia Deserta,* edited by Edward Garnett (New York: Scribner's, 1908), "Doughty."

Specifics about life in late-thirteenth-century Venice, what it looked like, and the design of galleys and junks are historically accurate. As for Marco's personal experiences and what he felt about them, I wrote what I imagined based on the experiences of others in similar circumstances.

The quote on page 259 is from Marco Barbaro's account of the Polo family. It appears in Y-C, Introduction, vol. 1, p. 25.

NOTES

Marco Polo lived from 1254 to 1324. He lived seventy years—a remarkably long life for his time, proof that he was both tough and lucky. So far as we know, he was only sick once—in the mountains approaching the Pamir Plateau.

He left Venice in November 1271, age seventeen, and arrived at Xanadu, Kublai's summer palace in Mongolia, three and a half years later, in May 1275. He served in Kublai's court for seventeen years, until 1292, and arrived back in Venice in 1295. Captured in a sea fight with the Genoese in September 1298, he was held prisoner until August 1299. In captivity he told his adventures to a writer of popular romances named Rustichello, who wrote what we know variously as *Marco Polo's Marvels, The Book of Travels,* or *Description of the World.*

Chapter 1, Packing Light: "Amongst the explorers to whom we owe such knowledge as we possess about the Gobi, the most important have been Marco Polo . . ."—*Encyclopedia Britannica,* 11th ed. (1910–11), "Gobi," vol. 12, p. 165.

Chapter 2, Marco Polo's Hilton: I first encountered the carved red camel in Salley Vickers's *Miss Garnet's Angel* (New York: HarperCollins, 2000).

Mark heard Antonio Vivaldi's "Four Seasons" in the café.

Many buildings in Venice slant because the oak, ash, and elm pilings they're built upon have settled into the island mud over the years. A good description of Venetian building techniques with excellent illustrations is in the *Eyewitness Travel Guide: Venice and the Veneto* (London: DK Publishing, 2004), pp. 20–21.

Chapter 3, Marco Polo's Pillow: For more about Venetian galleys, see Y-C, Introduction, vol. 1, section 5, "Digression concerning the war-galleys of the Mediterranean States in the Middle Ages," pp. 31–41, and Frederic Chapin Lane's *Venetian Ships and Shipbuilders of the Renaissance* (Baltimore: Johns Hopkins University Press, 1934), chap. 1, "The Galleys," particularly pp. 7–13.

Chapter 4, The Wheezing Sickness: A gripping description of asthma and the history of its treatment is in David McCullough's biography of Teddy Roosevelt, *Mornings on Horseback* (New York: Simon and Schuster, 1981).

I've imagined Boss based on Marco's description of Kublai's mastiffs: Y-C, vol. 1, chap. 19, "Concerning [those] who have charge of the Khan's hounds," pp. 400–401. Elsewhere he remarks that the Tibetan shamans were accompanied by "the very largest mastiff dogs in the world, which are as large as asses and are very good at catching all sorts of wild beasts" (Bergreen, p. 175).

Chapter 5, The School of the Street: Marco Polo mentions "apples of Paradise" in book 1, chap. 18 (p. 97 in the Y-C edition, and see note 1 to that chapter, p. 99). For more on this subject, see Beryl Brintnall Simpson and Molly Connor Ogorzaly's "Citrus Fruits" in *Economic Botany: Plants in Our World* (New York: McGraw Hill, 1995), p. 121.

"The Silk Road" is the modern name given to a veining of trade routes that went from what we know today as the Chinese city of Xi'an, some by northern routes, some by southern, to entrepôts on the Black and Mediterranean Seas. For a contemporary description, see Thubron, p. 3.

Did Marco Polo go to China? Some scholars, like Frances Wood in *The Silk Road: Two Thousand Years in the Heart of Asia* (Berkeley: University of California Press, 2002), say he didn't. They think he made up his story from other travelers' accounts. If he did, he wove silk from straw.

I think Marco did go to Xanadu, and on to China. *The Travels* doesn't feel like something worked up from other writers' scraps. All those extraordinary details are like whorls in a fingerprint, unique and compelling right from the start with Marco's coming-home story. Where had he been for such a long time? We also know from official records that when the Polos arrived at the Black Sea port of Trebizond on their way home, the Genoese took some of their cargo. Where had they been?

No pictures of Marco Polo are known to have been made during his lifetime. See Y-C, Introduction, p. 75.

To get some idea of what Marco's schooling might have been like, see John Larner's *Marco Polo and the*

Discovery of the World (New Haven: Yale University Press, 1999), p. 37.

I've imagined Mustafa, although I'm pretty sure Marco learned about China from someone—or several—like him in the school of the street. Doughty suggested to me his advice to Marco and some of his expressions.

For the desert pirates' attack and their magical devilish darkness of dry fog, see Y-C, vol. 1, book 1, chap. 18, and note 4 to that chapter. These are also described in M-P, p. 122.

Concerning Ladino, the traders' language, see Max Weinreich, *History of the Yiddish Language* (New Haven: Yale University Press, 2008).

Chapter 7, Marco's Homecoming: The story of the Polos' return to Venice is given in Y-C, vol. 1, "Personal History of the Travellers," p. 25.

The gold stick that served the Polos as money and passport—"paiza of the Mongols"—is pictured on the inside cover of Y-C, vol. 1.

Chapter 8, Marco Goes Crazy: The gambit is described in Y-C, vol. 1, "Personal History of the Travellers," p. 25.

Chapter 9, Stealing the Bones: In my imagining, both Mark's father and Dr. Hornaday were in Kirkuk together during the Gulf War. For an account of Hussein's 1988 gas attack, see "Dedicated Group Hopes to Prove Chemicals Killed Kurds," *The New York Times,* International Section, June 25, 2006, p. 4.

I've taken liberties with what is known about the Venetian merchants who collected Saint Mark's relics. For a bare-bones account, see Patrick Geary's *Furta Sacra: Thefts of Relics in the Central Middle Ages* (Princeton: Princeton University Press, 1978).

The guidebooks I've used are *Venice and the Veneto* (London: DK Publishing, Inc., 2004) and Alta Macadam's *Blue Guide Venice* (London: Somerset Books, 2007).

Chapter 10, Blindman's Bluff: The medieval Europeans' conception of "dog-headed men" probably came from travelers' descriptions of Chinese temple guardians—hideous terra-cotta grotesques glazed green and brown with fists raised in fury, the screaming heads twisted upward.

As for the idea of silk growing on trees, perhaps an early traveler saw a cocoon on a mulberry tree and figured it was some sort of fruit or seed. For centuries the cultivation of silk was a closely guarded secret to protect China's most valuable export. In terms of value and volume, silk was the principal commodity carried on the road.

The working of silk goes back more than six thousand years. Colin Thubron reports that a Neolithic carver scratched the image of a silkworm on an ivory cup and that other early sites have yielded red silk ribbon. His tellings of the legend of Lei-tzu discovering silk and the silk moth's tragic life are vivid (Thubron, pp. 4, 124–126). On pages 124–126 he tells how silk is prepared.

Chapter 11, A Secret Mission: I think the doge sent the Polos to Kublai. Some authorities say they sent themselves as merchants; others think it was the pope—for example, William Dalrymple in "The Venetian Treasure Hunt," a review of *Venice and the Islamic World, 828–1797,* an exhibition at the Metropolitan Museum of Art, New York, *New York Review of Books,* July 19, 2007, pp. 29–31.

About my hunch that Jewish merchants helped the Polos, see Benjamin Arbel's *Trading Nations: Jews and Venetians in the Early Modern Eastern Mediterranean* (New York: E. J. Brill, 1995). Amitav Ghosh's *In an An-*

tique Land (New York: Alfred A. Knopf, 1993) tells the story of Abraham Ben Yiju, a twelfth-century Jewish trader in a network that ran from Egypt to India. For other accounts see S. D. Goitein's *Letters of Medieval Jewish Traders* (Princeton: Princeton University Press, 1973).

The money letters that the thirteenth-century merchant-financiers sent to one another were a means for a buyer in one place to arrange for payment from funds far distant without having to ship specie. See Frederic C. Lane and Reinhold C. Mueller's *Money and Banking in Medieval and Renaissance Venice* (Baltimore: Johns Hopkins University Press, 1985); Mueller's *The Venetian Money Market: Banks, Panics, and the Public Debt, 1200–1500* (Baltimore: Johns Hopkins University Press, 1997); and Edmund B. Fryde's *Studies in Medieval Trade and Finance* (London: Hambledon Press, 1983).

For information about Mongol maps, see Jack Weatherford's *Genghis Khan and the Making of the Modern World* (New York: Three Rivers Press, 2004), especially chap. 9, "The Golden Light," pp. 222–223.

Chapter 12, How Marco's Story Got Told: Concerning Islamic calligraphy, see Sheila S. Blair's *Islamic Calligraphy* (Edinburgh: Edinburgh University Press, 2006).

For a more general discussion of the art of Islam, E. H. Gombrich's *The Story of Art* (Englewood Cliffs, New Jersey: Prentice-Hall, Inc., 1984) has an excellent brief discussion, "Looking Eastwards," chap. 7 in the 14th edition.

For information about the immense Chinese junks and the compass used by Oriental navigators, see Mansel Davies's *A Selection from the Writings of Joseph Needham,* edited by Mansel Davies (London: McFarland & Company, 1994), specifically "China, Europe, and the Seas Between," pp. 166–177; and Sean McGrail's "Marco Polo" in *Boats of the World from the Stone Age to Medieval Times* (London: Oxford University Press, 2001), section 10.6, pp. 377–381.

The sea fight with Genoa probably took place in 1298. It is described in Frederic C. Lane's *Venetian Ships and Shipbuilders of the Renaissance* (Baltimore: Johns Hopkins University Press, 1934).

For more about the battle and Marco's capture and how Marco's book got written, see Y-C, Introduction, p. 6; section 6, "The Jealousies and Naval Wars of Venice and Genoa," pp. 41–55; and section 7, "Rusticiano or Rustichello of Pisa, Marco Polo's Fellow-Prisoner at Genoa, the Scribe Who Wrote Down the Travels," pp. 55–64.

For more about different versions and editions of *The Travels,* see John Larner's *Marco Polo and the Discovery of the World* (New Haven: Yale University Press, 1999), pp. 3–7, 58.

Concerning the nickname "Marco Milione" and the Venetian masque figures, see Y-C, Introduction, pp. 67–68.

Chapter 13, To the Court of Kublai Khan: I've drawn some of the desert detail from Doughty and Lawrence. Both borrowed from Marco's telling.

The account of mountain travel with yaks and the setting I've used for my description of Marco recovering from his illness are drawn from Shor. The gap-vaulting yak is hers.

Marco's description of the post stations and bell-wearing runners is taken from M-P, pp. 242–245.

Chapter 14, Marco Meets Kublai: Xanadu and Kublai's tent palace are described in Y-C, vol. 1, book 1, chap. 61, pp. 298–304, and see notes 2–5, pp. 304–308.

Marco's description of the humbling bar is taken from M-P, p. 219. His illness approaching the Pamir highlands is taken from M-P, p. 142. For a map, see Y-C, vol. 1, "Marco Polo Itineraries," no. 3, pp. 178–179.

Concerning the stitched vessels the Polos spurned, see Y-C, vol. 1, chap. 19, and note 3, pp. 117–119. A useful feature of such craft was their flexibility—they were not as likely to break up landing in surf as was a more rigid spike-secured plank vessel. For more about them, see Sean McGrail's *Boats of the World from the Stone Age to Medieval Times,* section 6.7.3, pp. 269–272.

As for the unhealthy heat and deadly winds of Hormuz—"a very sickly place," in Marco's words—see Y-C, vol. 1, book 1, chap. 19, note 4, pp. 119–120, and note 5, p. 120, "History of Hormuz," note 6, pp. 120–121.

Hormuz and the sewn plank boats are also described in M-P, pp. 123–125.

Oil for camel itch: See Y-C, vol. 1, book 1, chap. 3, p. 46, and note 5 on p. 49 about the "springs of naphtha" on the Baku Peninsula on the Caspian Sea "supplying the whole country as far as Baghdad." The itch was probably mange.

The village wiped out by Kublai's grandfather may have been Balkh. See Thubron, pp. 234–235.

Chapter 15, On the Gobi: For more about the oasis wells and their purging salts, see Y-C, vol. 1, book 1, chap. 20, p. 123, and note 2 on p. 124.

The story of the camel following the pelt of her dead calf is taken from Lawrence, p. 247.

Marco's description of the shrines at Dunhuang is in M-P, pp. 150–159.

Chapter 16, A Great Miracle: For Marco on paper money, see M-P, pp. 238–240, and Jonathan M. Bloom, *Paper Before Print* (New Haven: Yale University Press, 2001), pp. 139–141.

Chapter 17, His Impertinence Beards the Emperor: The Marco Milione mask and its use in the Venetian masques is noted in Y-C, Introduction, p. 67. Koumiss is fermented mares' milk. It is nourishing, effervescent, unpleasantly pungent, and somewhat alcoholic. For more about it, see Y-C, vol. 1, "Kimiz or Kumiz," note 2 to chapter 53, pp. 259–260.

The eye ointment Marco describes—"tutty"—we know as zinc oxide. Marco's account is given in Y-C, vol. 1, book 1, chap. 21, p. 125, and see note 2, p. 126.

Solomon's dream is recounted in I Kings 3:9.

Chapter 18, The Wonders of China: For more about Chinese astronomy and the preparation of the all-important almanacs, see Nathan Sivin's *Granting the Seasons: The Chinese Astronomical Reform of 1280, with an Annotated Translation and Study of Its Many Dimensions.* I am grateful to Dr. Sivin for sharing with me an early draft of parts of his book concerning Kublai's interest in astronomy in connection with preparing the Chinese calendar and his reliance on Muslim astronomists to help read heavenly signs and portents.

For a description of how Marco's *Travels* inspired Columbus, see S. E. Morison's *Admiral of the Ocean Sea: A Life of Christopher Columbus* (Boston: Little, Brown and Company, Inc., 1942), pp. 64–69, 237–238, and Y-C, Introduction, p. 106.

Marco never mentions taking notes as he traveled, and none have turned up, but I think he must have, so I've imagined his method.

Burial rites are described in M-P, pp. 151–152.

Kublai's secret garden and Marco's contributions are my conjecture. For more about his elephants, see M-P, pp. 210–211.

Marco's description of Kublai's priest is given in Y-C, book 1, chap. 61, pp. 301–303, and see notes 8–10, pp. 309–314.

Kublai also employed Kashmirian conjurers. These are described in Y-C, book 1, chap. 31, and see note 2, p. 168.

The story of the sparrow in the castle is based on

the Venerable Bede's *Ecclesiastical History of the English People*. The speech in favor of Christianity is by one of King Edwin's Saxon noblemen. Professor Michèle Mulcahey, Department of Medieval History, School of History, University of St. Andrews, suggested this when I asked her how Marco might have described his faith to Kublai.

The stories Marco tells Kublai are drawn not in order from the Y-C edition of *The Travels.*

The capture of Baghdad story is in Y-C, book 1, chap. 6, "Of the Great City of Baudas, and How It Was Taken," pp. 63–68. I've added my imagining of the battle to Marco's account.

Chapter 19, The Plot: Kublai suffered from gout—the accumulation of crystals of ureic acid around the joints (usually in the feet)—for which, as then, there is no sure remedy, although a change of diet can help (reduced protein, simpler food), and certain drugs can be prescribed to reduce the body's tendency to accumulate ureic acid.

The fine dust Marco encountered is called loess, a kind of silt that forms a fertile topsoil in several parts of the world.

I've imagined the plot and the confrontation with Kublai.

Chapter 20, Escape!: The story is given in Y-C, vol. 1, "Prologue," chaps. 17–18, pp. 31–37.

For more about the Strait of Malacca, see Peter Gwin's "Dangerous Straits," *National Geographic,* vol. 212, no. 4 (October 2007), p. 126.

Noble Mauricio, the princess's gray donkey, does not appear in *The Travels.* He owes his presence and some of his habits to Mary Ellen Chase's *The Golden Asse and Other Essays* (New York: Henry Holt & Co, 1929).

Concerning cholera, see Sandra Hempel's *The Medical Detective: John Snow and the Mystery of Cholera* (London: Grantia Books, 2006).

SELECTED BIBLIOGRAPHY

Arbel, Benjamin. *Trading Nations: Jews and Venetians in the Early Modern Eastern Mediterranean.* New York: E. J. Brill, 1995.

Ashtor, Eliyahu. *The Levant Trade in the Later Middle Ages.* Princeton: Princeton University Press, 1983.

Bergreen, Laurence. *Marco Polo: From Venice to Xanadu.* New York: Alfred A. Knopf, 2007.

Blair, Sheila S. *Islamic Calligraphy.* Edinburgh: Edinburgh University Press, 2006.

Bloom, Jonathan M. *Paper Before Print.* New Haven: Yale University Press, 2001.

Carboni, Stefano. "Moments of Vision: Venice and the Islamic World 828–1797," introduction to exhibition catalog, *Venice and the Islamic World, 828–1797.* New York: Metropolitan Museum of Art, 2007, 12–35.

Chanda, Nayan. *Bound Together: How Traders, Preachers,*

Adventurers, and Warriors Shaped Globalization. New Haven: Yale University Press, 2007.

Cipolla, Carlo M. *Before the Industrial Revolution: European Society and Economy, 1000–1700.* New York: W. W. Norton & Company, Inc., 1976.

Davies, Mansel, ed. *A Selection from the Writings of Joseph Needham.* London: McFarland & Company, Inc., 1994.

Dear, I. C. B., and Peter Kemp, eds. *The Oxford Companion to Ships and the Sea,* 2nd ed. London: Oxford University Press, 2007.

Doughty, Charles M. *Travels in Arabia Deserta.* Edited by Edward Garnett. New York: Scribner's, 1908.

Edwards, Mike, and Michael Yamashita. "The Adventure of Marco Polo." *National Geographic,* vol. 7, no. 5 (May 2001).

Evans, Helen C., ed. *Byzantium: Faith and Power (1261–1557).* New York: Metropolitan Museum of Art, 2004.

Forster, E. M. "Marco Polo" in *Abinger Harvest.* New York: Harcourt Brace, 1936.

Geary, Patrick J. *Furta Sacra: Thefts of Relics in the Central Middle Ages.* Princeton: Princeton University Press, 1978.

Ghosh, Amitav. *In an Antique Land.* New York: Alfred A. Knopf, 1992.

Goitein, S. D. *A Mediterranean Society.* Berkeley: University of California Press, 1967.

———. *Letters of Medieval Jewish Traders.* Princeton: Princeton University Press, 1974.

Gwin, Peter. "Dangerous Straits: Dark Passage: The Strait of Malacca." *National Geographic,* vol. 212, no. 4 (October 2007).

Hart, Henry H. *Marco Polo: Venetian Adventurer.* Norman: University of Oklahoma Press, 1967.

Haw, Stephen G. *Marco Polo's China: A Venetian in the Realm of Khubilai Khan.* New York: Routledge, 2006.

Hildebrand, J. R. "The World's Greatest Overland Explorer." *National Geographic,* vol. 54 (November 1928), pp. 505–568.

Hutchinson, Gillian. *Medieval Ships and Shipping.* Rutherford, NJ: Fairleigh Dickinson University Press, 1994.

Kiple, Kenneth F. A *Movable Feast: Ten Millennia of Food Globalization.* Cambridge: Cambridge University Press, 2007.

Lane, Frederic C. *Venetian Ships and Shipbuilders of the Renaissance.* Baltimore: Johns Hopkins University Press, 1934.

Lane, Frederic C., and Reinhold C. Mueller. *Money and Banking in Medieval and Renaissance Venice,* vol. 2. Baltimore: Johns Hopkins University Press, 1985.

Larner, John. *Marco Polo and the Discovery of the World.* New Haven: Yale University Press, 1999.

Lattimore, Owen. *High Tartary.* New York: AMS Press, 1975.

Lawrence, T. E. *Revolt in the Desert.* London: Jonathan Cape, 1927.

Lopez, Robert S. *The Commercial Revolution of the Middle Ages.* Cambridge: Cambridge University Press, 1976.

"Marco Polo," *Encyclopedia Britannica,* 11th ed., vol. 22. 711. Cambridge: Cambridge University Press, 1911.

Martin, Lillian Ray. *The Art and Archaeology of Venetian Ships and Boats.* College Station: Texas A&M University, 2001.

McCullough, David. *Mornings on Horseback.* New York: Simon and Schuster, 1981.

McGrail, Sean. *Boats of the World: From the Stone Age to Medieval Times.* London: Oxford University Press, 2001.

Meskill, John T., ed. *An Introduction to Chinese Civilization.* Lexington, Massachusetts: D. C. Heath and Company, 1973. See especially chap. 6, "An Era of Foreign Rule," pp. 147–156, "The Yuan Dynasty (1260–1368)."

Morison, Samuel Eliot. *Admiral of the Ocean Sea: A Life of Christopher Columbus.* Boston: Little, Brown and Company, Inc., 1942.

Mueller, Reinhold C. *The Venetian Money Market: Banks, Panics, and the Public Debt, 1200–1500.* Baltimore: Johns Hopkins University Press, 1997.

National Geographic Society. *Atlas of the World,* rev. 6th ed. Washington, DC: National Geographic Society, 1992.

Needham, J., and W. Ling. *Science and Civilisation in China.* vol. 3, p. 681. Cambridge: Cambridge University Press, 1956.

Needham, Joseph. "The Epic of Gunpowder and Firearms, Developing from Alchemy" in *Science in Traditional China: A Comparative Perspective,* pp. 27–56. Cambridge, Massachusetts: Harvard University Press, 1981.

Norwich, John Julius. *A Short History of Byzantium.* New York: Alfred A. Knopf, 1999.

Olschki, Leonardo. *Marco Polo's Asia: An Introduction to His Description of the World.* Berkeley: University of California Press, 1960.

Osborne, John. "Politics, Diplomacy and the Cult of Relics in Venice and the Northern Adriatic in the First Half of the Ninth Century." In *Early Medieval Europe,* vol. 8, chap. 3, 369–386. Oxford: Blackwell Publishers, Ltd., 2000.

Polo, Marco. *The Travels.* Yule-Cordier ed. 2 vols. New York: Dover Publications, 1993.

Rossabi, Morris. *Khubilai Kahn: His Life and Times.* Berkeley: University of California Press, 1988.

Roth, C. *History of Jews in Venice.* Philadelphia: Jewish Publication Society of America, 1930.

Schoeser, Mary. *Silk.* New Haven: Yale University Press, 2007.

Shor, Jean Bowie. *After You, Marco Polo.* New York: McGraw-Hill Book Company, Inc., 1955.

Simpson, Beryl Brintnall, and Molly Connor Ogorzaly. "Citrus Fruits." *Economic Botany: Plants in Our World,* 2nd ed. New York: McGraw Hill, Inc., 1995.

Sivin, Nathan. *Granting the Seasons: The Chinese Astronomical Reform of 1280, with an Annotated Translation and Study of Its Many Dimensions. Sources and Studies in the History of Mathematics and Physical Sciences.* Secaucus, New Jersey: Springer, 2008.

Spufford, Peter. *Power and Profit: The Merchant in Medieval Europe.* London: Thames and Hudson, 2002.

Talbot, Richard. J. A., ed. *Barrington Atlas of the Greek and Roman World.* Princeton: Princeton University Press, 2000.

Thesiger, Wilfred. *Arabian Sands.* New York: Viking, 1959.

Thubron, Colin. *Shadow of the Silk Road.* New York: HarperCollins, 2007.

Venice and the Islamic World, 828–1797. New Haven: Yale University Press, 2007.

Weatherford, Jack. *Genghis Khan and the Making of the Modern World.* New York: Three Rivers Press, 2004.

Yamashita, Michael. *Marco Polo: A Photographer's Journey.* Vercelli, Italy: White Star Publishers, 2002.

Acknowledgments

I'm grateful for help received from the late G.R.D. Bridson of the Hunt Institute, Pittsburgh; Mr. William T. Brown; Ms. Leslie Button, associate director for collection services, W.E.B. Du Bois Library, University of Massachusetts, Amherst; Constance J. Covington, MD; Mr. Johnny Chung of Shanghai Far East Expeditions, Inc.; Ms. Abigail Dallmann; Dr. Walter S. Denny, professor of Islamic art, University of Massachusetts, Amherst; Ms. Kristen Depken, then editorial assistant, Random House Children's Books; Ms. Gina Douglas, executive officer, archivist and librarian emeritus, the Linnean Society of London; Mr. Jonathan Flaccus; Dr. Carmella Franklin, director, American Academy in Rome; Dr. Michael Gasster, professor of history emeritus, Rutgers University; Dr. Patrick Geary, 2006 resident scholar, American Academy in Rome; Ms. Meika

Hashimoto, editorial assistant, Random House, New York; Dr. Robert L. Herbert, professor emeritus of humanities, Mount Holyoke College; Ms. Marcie Hermansader; Mrs. Mary Hill; Mr. Leonid Lerman; Dr. Joseph Mandell; Dr. Anna Marguerite McCann; Mr. James McCormick; Ms. Faith P. Moeckel; Dr. Michèle Mulcahey, Department of Medieval History, School of History, University of St. Andrews; Ms. Christine Pagnani, Academic Arrangements Abroad; Ms. Diane H. Schafer, Metropolitan Museum of Art; Dr. Nathan Sivin, professor emeritus of Chinese studies and the history of science, University of Pennsylvania; Dr. Ross Terrill, research associate, Fairbanks Center for Asian Research, Harvard University; and the wonderful research librarians at the Neilson Library, Smith College, Northampton, Massachusetts.

About the Author

Alan Armstrong went to China to see what Marco Polo might have seen, flying in one day the distance it took Marco three years to go by galley, camel, yak, horse, and foot, nearly at the cost of his life. Inspired by Polo's hunger for exploration and his gift for describing what he met, Armstrong wrote *Looking for Marco Polo,* his third book for children. His first book, *Whittington,* was awarded a Newbery Honor in 2006. He lives with his wife, Martha, a painter, in Massachusetts.